read

Blaze™

Dear Reader,

Back when I used to be a freelance journalist, one of my jobs was to interview every one of the Vancouver Canucks for a feature in their magazine. It was a great gig. I got to meet the players and often their wives and families in their homes and really got a sneak peek at what their lives are like off the ice and out of the spotlight. The truth? Most of them were nice family men who happen to have a really great job. Oh, yeah, they were also fit, tall and hot!

When I started to write *Face-Off*, I wanted to give a sense of a hockey family, so I created two smoking-hot hockey-playing brothers and a sister who's always had to be a little bit tough to keep up with them. Naturally, each of them will be challenged both on and off the ice as they face their fears and find love—whether they are looking for it or not.

I hope you enjoy *Face-Off*. As always, I love to hear from you. Come visit me on the web at www.nancywarren.net.

Happy reading,

Nancy Warren

Nancy Warren

FACE-OFF

TORONTO NEW YORK LONDON
AMSTERDAM PARIS SYDNEY HAMBURG
STOCKHOLM ATHENS TOKYO MILAN MADRID
PRAGUE WARSAW BUDAPEST AUCKLAND

Recycling programs
for this product may
not exist in your area.

ISBN-13: 978-0-373-79601-4

FACE-OFF

Copyright © 2011 by Nancy Warren

ABOUT THE AUTHOR

USA TODAY bestselling author Nancy Warren lives in the Pacific Northwest, where her hobbies include walking her border collie in the rain and following her favorite hockey team. She's the author of more than thirty novels and novellas for Harlequin and has won numerous awards. Visit her website at www.nancywarren.net.

Books by Nancy Warren

HARLEQUIN BLAZE
19—LIVE A LITTLE!
47—WHISPER
57—BREATHLESS
85—BY THE BOOK
114—STROKE OF MIDNIGHT
     "Tantalizing"
209—PRIVATE RELATIONS
275—INDULGE
389—FRENCH KISSING
452—UNDER THE INFLUENCE
502—POWER PLAY
526—TOO HOT TO HANDLE
553—MY FAKE FIANCÉE
569—THE EX FACTOR

HARLEQUIN SUPERROMANCE
1390—THE TROUBLE WITH TWINS

Don't miss any of our special offers. Write to us at the following address for information on our newest releases.

Harlequin Reader Service
U.S.: 3010 Walden Ave., P.O. Box 1325, Buffalo, NY 14269
Canadian: P.O. Box 609, Fort Erie, Ont. L2A 5X3

For my very own knight
in (sometimes) shining armor. With love.

Ice Time

1

"ONE MORE TIME, BIG J, scrape that blade down your face and look into the camera like this is the greatest shave of your life," the enthusiastic director instructed him as though this was the first take of the shaving commercial and not the eighth.

Jarrad McBride experienced a flash of annoyance. He knew the guy was only doing his job, but he hated being called Big J. It was a hockey-player nickname, and he wasn't a hockey player anymore. What he was, was a guy who peddled shaving cream and toothpaste on TV. He had no idea why anybody would buy shaving cream 'cause a guy who used to shoot pucks down the ice appeared on their flat screen and told them to, but he'd long ago worked out that the world was a crazy place, and L.A. was the epicenter of crazy.

"If you keep him lathered up much longer he's going to get a rash," Lester Salisbury said. Lester was his manager and the reason for all these "promotional opportunities." He was smart and knew Jarrad well enough that he'd picked up on the annoyance, even if he'd misinterpreted the cause.

"That's okay, Les. If I got paid this much money every time I shaved, I'd be a wealthy man."

"You're already a wealthy man," Les reminded him as the young woman whose job it was to display the cream to best advantage on his face danced up and smoothed the edges with careful finger swirls as though she was icing a cake.

She was pretty, with flyaway blond hair and innocent blue eyes. Jarrad should hit on her, he knew that. Partly because of his reputation and also because of the way she'd shot a couple of half scared, half hopeful glances at him; she obviously expected it. He didn't want to let her down, but he really didn't have the energy.

Still, he didn't want to hurt her feelings. "Thanks, Jill," he said.

Her eyes widened. "You remembered my name?"

In fact, he had a great memory, he remembered the names of a lot of people he'd like to forget as well as his near and dear, and when people drifted in and out of his life—as an astonishing number seemed to do—he tried to pay attention at least while they were in his orbit.

Jill seemed like a nice enough girl, but he could see she'd bore him in an evening. He suspected that if she didn't get hit on by a guy of his reputation, she'd take it the wrong way. "How could I forget someone who takes care of me so well," he said, smiling. Then, for the ninth time, he picked up the razor and stared into the movie camera.

Todd, the director, said, "And three, and two and one," and on cue Jarrad scraped the blade slowly down his face.

"Great," Todd said with as much enthusiasm as if he'd just played Hamlet on Broadway to a standing ovation. "Now, we'll get you shaved and then we'll do your speaking part." Jill toweled the white stuff off his face.

A professional barber was waiting for him in the film studio's dressing room. Personally, he thought it was cheating to pretend that one brand of shaving cream could give as good a look as a pro, but, as Les often reminded him, nobody paid him to think.

"Looking good, buddy," his manager said as he walked him down the hall.

Once he'd been shaved, moisturized and hair-styled, the makeup woman tried to dab makeup on his scar, but he put up a hand to stop her. "That scar's my trademark, honey. You cover that up, people'll wonder what else you're hiding."

Luckily, Todd sided with him, so he was allowed to finish the shoot looking at least a little bit like himself.

The enthusiasm was as thick as the shaving cream when the director prepared him for his pitch. "Remember, you believe in this product. When you say your lines, think about something that really excites you."

"Okay." Sounded easy enough to think of something that excited him. He searched. His mind was blank. He could think about sex but that only reminded him of the tabloid pictures of his ex-wife cavorting in Belize, letting the world know she'd traded up to the NBA.

He could think about his bank balance, but he knew he'd never be able to spend all his money no matter how long he lived, which for some reason made him wonder how old he'd be when he kicked it. Another uninspiring thought.

Most of his greatest moments had happened in hockey rinks, but his retirement was still too raw, too unexpected. His mind veered away.

Finally he moved back to childhood, settled on a

memory of going to the pound and picking out a puppy when he was a kid. He and his sister both went, his baby brother not being thought of yet, and even though they argued about everything, they'd instantly agreed on the eager-looking young black Lab who'd squirmed and danced with excitement at their visit, licking their faces and making them all laugh. He'd wanted to call the dog Lucky, Samantha argued for Lucy and somehow they ended up calling the dog Fred.

Maybe if he thought hard enough about Fred he could forget that this shaving cream dialogue was butt-awful.

While Fred galloped through his memory, racing after a Frisbee, stick, ball, puck, rock, sock, pretty much anything that moved, Jarrad looked right into that big square camera, ignoring the camera operator, the beaming director, his hovering manager, the lighting guy, the sound guy and the gophers. He saw Fred leap into the air, teeth closing on a badly chewed and mangled red Frisbee, his black body wriggling in happiness and said, "A perfect shave is like a skating rink right before the action. Smooth, clean, cool. Like my shaving cream." As instructed he now glanced at the blue canister in his hand and back at the camera. "Ice."

He'd refused to let them film him anywhere near a hockey rink or the equipment of a game he could no longer play. Instead, they'd hired a good-looking female model and shot the pair of them supposedly heading out for a night on the town. They'd already shot all that stuff earlier. Once Todd was happy with his one line, he'd be out of here.

It took two more tries, and Fred dragged rocks out of the creek down by their old house before Todd called it a wrap.

He shook hands with everybody, flirted with the

shaving cream girl a little bit more, and finally he and Les were free. As they hit the pavement both pulled out similar black shades and slipped them on against the glare of an endlessly sunny L.A. day. "Two days to film a thirty-second commercial?" he complained, as though he'd never done one before.

"I should make your hourly wage," Les said.

"It was boring."

Les patted him awkwardly on the shoulder. "I know it's tough now that you've had to hang up your skates. And stuff." A delicate silence hung in the air, but they both knew that *and stuff* referred to his ex making a fool of him in public. "You have to do something with your time," he reminded him.

And that was the problem.

He'd have countered with some smart-assed remark except that his new smart phone rang. And call display told him it was somebody he actually wanted to talk to. Unlike Les, on the subject of what he was going to do with his life.

"I was just thinking about Fred," he said into the phone, waving goodbye to his agent as he did so.

Greg Olsen, his oldest friend in the world laughed. "He was the greatest dog. Except that he ran off with all our baseballs."

Jarrad adjusted his shades against the neverending sunshine of L.A. He still missed real winters and, amazingly enough, he even missed the Vancouver rain. "So, what's up? How's cop business?"

Greg ignored the question. "I saw *eChat Canada* last night."

"Since when do you watch entertainment porn?"

"Since your ex is making a fool of you with some

seven-foot-tall ball jockey. She flashed a big engagement rock on TV."

It wasn't sadness or grief that made his teeth clench on his expensive dental work, it was the humiliation of being reminded he'd been that stupid. Dumb enough to fall for the face and body that were as fake as the nice-girl routine. "Don't worry about it. I'm over her. And you never liked her."

"Dude, nobody liked her."

"Yeah, call it my L.A. phase, hang around movie stars, marry a swimsuit model, get a house with a pool, start—"

"I'm glad you said that," his oldest friend interrupted. "L.A. was a phase. It's not you."

Even as he accepted that his friend was right, he wondered if he even knew what he was anymore. Or where he belonged.

"I need you to come home."

"What are you talking about? Is somebody sick? In trouble?"

"No. But here's the thing. I need you, man."

"What, you're gay now?"

"Funny. No. It's the big league game."

"Big league" only meant one thing to Jarrad. NHL. From which he was forever barred. He shook his head. His thinking was hardly ever muddled anymore. Mostly, the only effect of the career-ending hit he'd taken was that he'd lost his peripheral vision. He wasn't Big J anymore. He was an unemployed thirty-five-year-old man who had no idea what he was going to do with the rest of his life apart from shaving in public on camera. "Big league?"

"The World Police and Firefighter Games hockey championship," Greg said in a "duh" tone, as though there could be no other league of any importance.

"Right. Sure. Ah, if you want a ringer, I can't play hockey anymore. You know that."

"You can't catch crooks or fight fires, either. I don't want you on the team."

"Then what do you want?"

Jarrad beeped open the doors of his overpriced luxury sports car.

"We're the worst team in the league. It's humiliating. We have this big rivalry going with Portland and what we need is a coach. They told me I was crazy to try, but me and the boys, well, we want you to coach us."

Jarrad damned near dropped his fancy new phone. He'd thought shooting shaving cream commercials was as low as he was going to fall. But coaching a bunch of cops and firefighters for an amateur hockey league?

"I don't know how to coach," he said, playing for time.

"Sure you do. You can play, can't you? So practice your coaching skills on us. We're not paying you, so we can't complain."

"I don't know. I'm pretty busy."

"No, you're not. You're sitting around feeling sorry for yourself."

He could argue the point, but Greg wouldn't be fooled.

"I need to think about it."

"Come home, do a good thing. Get your life back."

"I can't."

"Think about it."

"I'm heading out into traffic," he lied. "Gotta go." And he flipped shut the phone. Then he got slowly into the car, let the hum of the engine and the air-conditioning system—which constantly adjusted itself to his preferred temperature—soothe him.

As if he'd go home to his rain-soaked town and coach a bunch of amateurs. Home. He wasn't sure if it was the images of Fred or the call from Greg, but suddenly he felt a twinge of homesickness. Which was weird. He used to go back a lot when his dad was alive, but Art McBride had died a couple of years back from a sudden heart attack. Shortly after that, his mom had moved to Vancouver Island. A nurse, she'd taken a demanding hospital position, which all the family understood was her way of dealing with the grief and loneliness.

Vancouver in February was cold, rainy and dreary, he reminded himself as the sun beat against his expensive shades and the engine purred obediently beneath him.

He headed out the coast road to his Malibu home. He'd grab a swim, call up a nice woman and go get some dinner. Enjoy the riches life had so generously given him. So he couldn't play hockey anymore. Big deal. He'd figure out something to do with the time hanging heavy on his hands.

Sam, his younger sister by three years, was busy with her law practice. Even though she bugged him all the time to leave L.A. and move back home, she had a full life. It wasn't as if she needed him.

And Taylor, the youngest McBride, was too busy trying to take the McBride spot in the NHL to have much time for his older, washed-up brother.

Be great to see them, though. Maybe he'd fly up for a quick weekend. See the family and a few old friends. Maybe when the weather was better.

But as his house came into view, he realized that his old buddy, Greg, wasn't the only one who wondered how he was doing now that his ex-wife was engaged to a new victim.

Paparazzi clogged the gated entrance to his home like rats packing a sewer.

He swore under his breath. Didn't stop to think. He swung the car around in a tight U and sped away from his own house cursing aloud.

A couple of miles down the road, he pulled over. Even in the perfectly controlled air-conditioning he was sweating. He knew from experience that for the few days he and his ex and her new guy were the love triangle du jour, he'd get no peace.

He didn't want to answer questions.

He didn't want to pretend everything was okay.

He didn't want to find himself stalked by cameras as he tried to go about his business.

Damn it, and damn Greg for knowing him so well. He wanted to go home.

He called his assistant to book him a flight to Vancouver and then he called Greg.

"I'll be there Monday. Where do you practice and what time?"

2

"COME ON, IT'LL BE FUN," Tamson insisted as Sierra Janssen hesitated on the brink of the ice rink.

"Fun for you, watching me fall on my butt in the cold. It's seven in the morning on a Saturday, my day off. I should be sleeping in."

"None of us are great skaters. Who cares? We get some exercise, laugh a lot and it turns out that there's a team of firefighters and cops practicing in the next rink. Being here is much better than sitting around feeling sorry for yourself."

But Sierra wasn't sure that sitting around feeling sorry for herself wouldn't, in fact, be more fun than attempting to play hockey when she hadn't skated in years. It was cold in here and smelled like old sweat socks. Colorful pennants hung from the impossibly high rafters boasting of wins and league championships. She'd passed a glass case of trophies telling similar stories. For some reason the word *league* only reminded her of Michael, who had been so far out of her league she'd never had a chance. What had a successful, handsome brain surgeon wanted with a grade-two schoolteacher who, on her best days, could only be termed *cute*. A good day at work for Michael was bringing someone out of a coma, cutting tumors out of brains. Her idea of success was getting seven-year-olds to put up their hands before asking a question.

No wonder he'd left her for an intern. In her bitter moments she thought it would have been nice if he'd had the courtesy to dump her first and not leave her to find out he was cheating in the most humiliating way. He'd sent her the hottest email. A sexual scorcher that left her eyes bugged open, it was so unlike him. He'd even used a pet name he'd never called her before. It wasn't until she'd read the email through a second time that she realized Jamie wasn't a pet name. It was the actual name of another woman. Who was clearly a lot wilder in bed than she would ever be.

The woman was training to be a doctor, scorching-hot in bed, a much better match for Michael.

She gritted her teeth. Okay, so her heart was broken. Tamson was right. She had to get out and embrace life, not sit around watching it happen to other people.

She'd loved skating when she was a kid. This would be fine. A fun league for women, no stress, she'd pick up her skating skills. Learn to play hockey. She'd played field hockey in high school and she'd been pretty darn good. What could be better?

She stepped a skate gingerly onto the ice. Hung on to the boards, stepped the other skate down.

Had the ice been this slippery when she was a child? Her ankles wobbled alarmingly in her rented skates and the padding she'd borrowed from her brother made her feel like the Michelin Man. On skates.

When she wobbled her way down the ice, holding her brother's old hockey stick, since he wouldn't trust her with his good one, joining the other women who were warming up, she realized that even here, in this fun hockey team for women, she was outclassed.

She was the only one who had to look at her skates to stay on the ice. And what she saw was that her legs were wide apart and she couldn't help but hold her arms out wide to stop herself from falling.

Somebody blew a whistle. "Okay, girls. Gather round."

JARRAD STOOD AT THE EDGE of the ice and realized his old buddy hadn't lied about the team. These guys were all over the place. Sure, some of them could skate, and the men were all fit, but there was no sense of teamwork, no idea how to sense where the puck was headed and what to do about it.

Not for the first time, he wondered what he was even doing here.

He was observing, he reminded himself, only observing. And what he observed didn't fill him with confidence in the team. He hadn't agreed to coach yet, maybe he'd take a pass.

"I'm going for a walk," he said to a grizzled old Norwegian who answered to Sig and was the closest thing to a coach the team currently had.

Sig nodded. "They're good guys, you know?"

"Sure. Probably great cops and firefighters, too." But any fool with functioning eyesight could see that getting this ragged bunch of men into shape as a team was going to take time, not to mention hard work and coaching skills Jarrad doubted he possessed. He wasn't sure there was enough time before the big league play-offs to get them into shape.

He stuffed his hands in his jeans and wandered. He'd spent so much of his life inside hockey rinks that he probably felt more comfortable in one than anywhere else on earth. He loved everything about the rink. The way it smelled like the inside of a fridge, the sound of skate blades scraping across ice, putting the first groove into the perfect surface right after the Zamboni finished. The guys. The team.

But there weren't skates on his feet now. And it wasn't him on the ice.

His sneakers were soundless as he headed down the hallway. At the next rink over he stopped to peer through the glass doors, and what he saw made him smile, genuinely smile, for the first time in months.

Without thinking, he opened the door and slipped inside.

On the ice was a group of women, ranging, he guessed from their twenties to their forties, all clad in mismatched hockey gear and helmets. This group made his firefighters seem like the hottest team in the NHL.

"You've got a breakaway. Sierra. Go!"

And he watched as a puck made its lazy way up the ice, at about the speed of a curling rock, and a slim young woman skated straight over to the boards and started up the rink.

She had to guess the direction of the puck, since she never took her eyes off her skates.

He moved closer. Put a foot up on a bench to watch. The breakaway got way past the cutie near the boards, and the goalie managed to stop it.

A whistle blew.

"Okay. Great work, ladies. See you all on Thursday."

And they all headed off the rink.

Except the woman with the breakaway. None of the other women had noticed she was now clinging to the boards like a burr to a dog. He got the feeling she was scared.

He gave her a minute and when she still hadn't budged, he stepped onto the ice.

Walked over to her.

"Hi," he said. "You need a hand?"

When her face turned up he felt a kind of shock travel through his system. He was so used to tanned bombshells that he'd forgotten how soft and pretty a woman could look. Beneath the helmet she had big blue eyes and pale skin. Blond hair that had picked up some static from the cold and was levitating in places.

"I don't think hockey's for me," she said.

He took the stick out of her hand and shot it across the ice toward the exit gate.

"Then you should probably get off the ice."

"I'm thinking about it."

He held out his hands, palms up. "Come on. Take my hand. I'll get you out of here."

She looked up at him. "What if we both fall?"

"I won't let you fall."

After thinking about it for a second, she gave him one hand.

"Your glove is too big," he said, feeling the smallness of her hands inside the huge mitt.

"I know. I borrowed all this stuff from my brother. Except for the skates."

"May I?" and without waiting for an answer, he pulled off her glove. And took her hand. Which was as small and soft as the rest of her seemed to be.

Once she knew he had her and he wasn't about to take her down, she held out her other hand. He pulled off the other glove, sent the pair skidding to join the stick, and then while she hung on with a death grip, walked slowly backward, sliding her along with him. "That's it."

Her cheeks were pink with cold and he sensed that, like her hands in those gloves, her body inside the padding was much smaller. "You need some equipment that fits you."

"No, I don't. I am done with hockey."

He laughed easily. Something he hadn't done in so long he'd almost forgotten the sound.

"I'm a coach. I could help you."

"That's sweet of you, but—"

"And here's your first lesson. Stop looking at your feet."

"But—"

"It's like dancing. You have to trust your body."

She glanced up, took a deep breath and skated forward a little bit. He let go of one hand and stepped to the side. "Now, relax and think about how good that cup of coffee's going to taste."

"What cup of coffee?"

"The one I'm going to buy you when we get off the ice."

She had dimples, he noticed when she smiled. "I don't even know your name."

He hesitated. It didn't seem like she'd recognized him. Now he was going to give her his name and that would ruin the fun vibe between them. "Jarrad."

She glanced up, and there wasn't the slightest recognition. "Hi, Jarrad. I'm Sierra."

"Pretty name. You're doing great, Sierra."

"It's easier when you hold me up."

"All you need is practice." As they reached the edge of the rink he was almost sorry. "And here we are." He helped her step off the ice, then went back to collect the gloves and stick.

When he returned, she was unlacing skates that in his opinion should be in the garbage. "Well? Can I buy you a coffee?"

She glanced at him, as though trying to divine his intention, which would be tough since he didn't know what his intentions were himself. Only that he liked the look of this woman and didn't want to say goodbye quite yet.

"All right."

Once she had her street shoes back on and the padding off, he realized he'd been correct. She had a sweet little body.

The coffee shop in the ice sports complex was quiet. He got them both a coffee and brought the steaming cups to the small table in the corner where he figured no hockey fans would spot him right away. Especially since he made sure to sit with his back to the room.

"You're tanned," she said. "Did you just get back from Hawaii or something?"

"California."

"Nice."

They sipped coffee and he realized he didn't have much practice anymore in talking to regular women who weren't either famous themselves or involved with celebrities.

While he racked his brain for something to say, she said, "What team do you coach?"

"Honestly, I'm not sure I'm going to coach them. It's the fire and police team, but I came here today as an observer and what I observed is there's no teamwork. No sense of a common goal. They're like a bunch of little kids, all trying to grab the glory."

A smile lit up her face. "Ah, maybe I can help. I know a lot about organizing little kids."

3

HE WAS SO CUTE, SIERRA thought, gazing at the earnest expression in the green eyes across from her. He had sun-streaked brown hair and a craggy face that was more appealing because it was so imperfect.

His nose had obviously been broken at least once and there was a toughness to his body that she liked. He had a scar that started at his left cheekbone, a little too close to the eye for her comfort in imagining what injury might have caused it, that jagged its way down an inch or so into his cheek. When he smiled, the scar creased like an overenthusiastic laugh line. She found it fascinating.

She'd never felt so comfortable with a man so quickly. It was as though she already knew him.

"I teach grade two. When the boys aren't getting along on the playing field, or aren't working together, you know what I do?"

He seemed absolutely fascinated. He leaned forward and cupped his chin in his hand. "What do you do?"

"You see, boys are very visual, and they're competitive. It's simply in their nature. So I tell them to imagine they are building a big fort. If each of them only looks out for himself, then there will be a bunch of little forts, none of them strong enough. But if they work together, they can build something stronger and better."

"And does it work?"

"Pretty well."

"Would it work with a bunch of overgrown boys? The kind who fight crime and put out fires?"

"I have no idea. But I've sometimes thought that when it comes to competition and games, big boys have a lot in common with little boys."

The man across from her laughed. "You know a lot about men."

"No," she said sadly. "I don't think I do."

He gazed at her quizzically for a moment, but instead of calling her on possibly the stupidest remark she'd ever made to an attractive stranger, he said, "I have an idea."

"What?"

"You help me with my overgrown kids and I'll teach you to skate well enough to be able to play hockey."

"I'm not sure I'm cut out for hockey," but to her own ears it sounded as if she was saying, "persuade me." And so he did.

"It's a fun sport, and if you want the respect of your young male pupils, tell them you play hockey. They'll think you rock."

She couldn't help a slightly smug smile from blooming. "My male students already think I rock."

When he smiled his whole face lit with charm. "That I can believe. I think my first love was my grade-two teacher. You know, those boys will still get dreamy-eyed about you decades from now. So, play hockey to push your boundaries."

"I'm not sure I want my boundaries pushed."

"All right, then. You and me, on the ice, right now, for thirty minutes. If, at the end of half an hour you don't want to continue, what have you lost? Half an hour of your time."

"Why would you want to teach me how to skate?"

"The truth is, I've never coached before. I think if I can get you interested in hockey, then maybe there's a chance I could actually be a coach." He drained the last of his coffee. "Besides, I like you. I want to spend more time with you."

She couldn't believe it. He announced interest in her as a woman as though it was a perfectly normal, everyday thing, not a big deal. And because he saw it that way, she was able to keep her own perspective.

She was pretty sure after half an hour dragging around the klutziest woman who had ever donned skates he'd be ready to call off his idea to teach her about hockey. But for half an hour, this interesting man was hers.

She nodded. "Okay."

"Great. Now, first thing we need to do is get you some skates."

"I have skates," she reminded him.

"Please. Wayne Gretzky couldn't skate in those things. They're trashed."

And he reached over and picked the dingy white boots up and strode out of the coffee shop with her trailing in his wake.

He received a flattering degree of attention from the rental place compared to how she'd fared. He must be a regular. And before long she was wearing a pair of proper hockey skates that definitely supported her ankles better. This time, when she stepped onto the ice, she felt more confident.

Jarrad ran back to the rink where the cops and firefighters were still practicing, returning with a sports bag. He pulled out his own skates. Mean-looking black things, which he laced up with incredible speed.

When they hit the ice, he took her hand. She couldn't believe how much she liked this, the holding hands, gliding across the frozen surface. Already she was feeling better.

"The first thing you have to do," he said, "is stop being so scared. You've got padding. So what if you fall? You'll slide. Get over it. The ice is your personal highway. Make friends with it."

Make friends with the ice?

She thought she might manage a nodding acquaintance, but at the end of half an hour she was skating. By herself. Without looking at her feet. He didn't call a halt and neither did she. Instead, he worked with her on a drill. He'd skate alongside her passing the puck, which she was able to retrieve most of the time.

She was having so much fun, she forgot to be scared. And that's when she fell. And slid.

She glanced up to find Jarrad gazing down at her.

She laughed. "You're right. It didn't hurt at all."

He held a hand down for her and helped her to her feet.

"So? You coming back for more?"

His hands rested on her shoulders and she felt some kind of sizzle run through all the layers of padding right to her skin. Coming back for more? Oh, yes, please.

She had no idea if he'd read her mind or was feeling the same sizzling attraction, but after looking at her for a moment, he said, "Have dinner with me tonight?"

"Dinner?" she said stupidly, as though she'd never heard the word.

"With me. Tonight."

She thought about refusing. For a nanosecond. There

was something about him, some confidence that suggested he might be one of those guys who was simply out of her league.

Then she thought of the way she'd spent the last hour. If she'd learned anything it was that sometimes when you fell it didn't hurt.

"I'd love to."

ONCE SHE GOT HOME, Sierra was determined to find something more flattering to wear than her brother's too-big hockey padding. She still couldn't believe that cute coach had asked her out. Or that she'd said yes.

She'd never been a spontaneous woman, and yet here she was—going out with a virtual stranger. In fact, she realized in horror, she didn't even know his last name.

But then she wasn't a complete fool. He didn't have hers either. They were meeting at the restaurant he'd named. One of the best restaurants in Vancouver, a west-coast seafood bistro in Yaletown that she only knew about because it had been written up so much. Not that she'd ever been there.

Of course, a restaurant like that demanded a certain amount of primping. If she'd had time she'd have bought a new dress, but she didn't have time for that, or a makeover. Or a six-week boot camp to get her body into peak shape. No, make that a fifty-six-week boot camp.

What she did have was a favorite little black dress, a new bottle of nail varnish in a hot designer color and a pair of Jimmy Choos she'd bought on sale because they were irresistible, though they were pricey even at fifty-percent off. Never had she been so happy that she hadn't listened to her sensible, frugal self on the day she'd spotted the green-and-black stilettos.

While she painted her nails, she flipped on the

television. She was channel surfing when she saw Jarrad. On her TV screen. For a second she thought she'd conjured him simply from thinking about him, but no, that really was Jarrad grinning out at her from her flat screen, with shaving cream all over his face.

She watched the entire commercial, a sick feeling spreading through her. The final image was of Jarrad with a woman who looked like a young Catherine Zeta Jones—all sex appeal and attitude—heading out on the town. She was as different from Sierra as Saks is from Wal-Mart. Nothing on that woman's body had come from the sales rack.

With a low moan of horror, Sierra realized that Jarrad was some kind of fancy hockey star. A couple of minutes on Google confirmed her worst fears.

This guy was so far out of her league they weren't even on the same planet.

An NHL superstar, he'd helped lead his team to Stanley Cup triumph three years ago. He'd taken a body blow to the head in an early-season game that had left him with some vision problems that meant he couldn't play professionally any more.

But far harder for her to stomach were the endless photographs of him with a stunning swimsuit model.

A swimsuit model, for heaven's sake. The kind of woman put on this earth to make Sierra forever feel like the forgettable girl next door.

What had she been thinking?

An aura of success had clung to him, she now realized. Everything from his tan to his easy charm to his uber-trendy jeans had screamed money. And look at the way they'd knocked themselves out at the skate-rental place.

How blind she'd been. How foolish. And why did she

keep setting herself up for failure with these men who were altogether too much for her?

But she hadn't done anything except cling to the boards like a motherless chimp to a tree. Why had he asked her out?

If only she had some way to get hold of him, she'd cancel their date.

Only she didn't.

So she simply wouldn't show up for their date. She'd call the restaurant and leave a message telling him she wasn't coming. Big deal. A superstar like that? He'd have a dinner companion five minutes after he sat himself down at the bar.

She looked up the restaurant's phone number. Picked up the phone. Put it down. Picked it up, put it down. A third time she picked the receiver up and then slammed the thing down. Sometimes Sierra cursed her mother for the manners she'd instilled in her daughter. No matter that Jarrad was way, way out of her league and was no doubt taking out a very ordinary primary-school teacher for obscure reasons of his own, she could not stand the man up on their first date.

It simply wasn't in her too-polite nature.

So, she tortured herself for a few more minutes by gazing at the perfect bikini-clad body of his professional-model former wife.

Not even her sexiest dress and the high heels could disguise the fact that Sierra's curves were modest at best, and her height no more than average.

She could argue that her face and body were entirely natural and kept in shape with regular yoga practice and sporadic jogging rather than discreet visits to a plastic surgeon, but pictures didn't lie. The former Mrs. McBride's nips and tucks and the vats of collagen Sierra suspected were responsible for that amazingly sexy pout were definitely doing their job.

Sierra picked up her evening bag and paused to glance in the mirror. One thing she was certain of—Jarrad McBride wouldn't be seeing her naked.

4

WHY DID HE KEEP picturing her naked? Jarrad could not figure it out. He wasn't the kind of guy to perv around a woman he barely knew. Besides, compared to the curvy babes in his regular world, Sierra wouldn't stand out.

And yet, he realized with most of the women he knew, it didn't take a lot of imagination to picture them naked. Sure a lot of them were gorgeous, some even that lucky by nature, but there was a kind of sameness to the big-breasted, long-limbed, long-haired, Chiclet-toothed, tanned females he'd been surrounded by in L.A.

Sierra was so different. Her curves were discreet. He doubted she even filled a B cup. Her hips weren't extravagantly full or boyishly slim, but somewhere in the middle. She wasn't tall or short, but average. And because the obvious places didn't grab all his attention, he found himself noticing how delicate her wrists were. How slim and elegant her neck. How much he liked the slight imperfection of her teeth when she smiled. One of her side teeth overlapped another, giving her a charming smile. Everything was so real with this woman.

Including her intelligence. Not that he wanted to put

down his ex, but her idea of news was to check Perez Hilton daily and pass on the bitchiest tidbits to him.

He'd asked for a private room in a restaurant he used to frequent, partly because of the upstairs space. Until he was no longer news, he really didn't want to be seen publicly. Not that the media in Vancouver were anything like the L.A. bunch, but he didn't want any problems. Besides, he didn't imagine Sierra wanted her photo on some gossip blog. She seemed to be a woman who liked her privacy. And who could blame her?

So, when the maître d' had escorted them upstairs to a private room, her eyes had widened for a moment but she hadn't commented.

Which made him explain.

"I'm sorry to do this to you, but there's been some media interest in me lately. I thought we might like some privacy."

She nodded. "I understand," she said softly. What a relief not to have to explain.

WELL, THE EVENING WAS going exactly as she would have imagined. He was already hiding her away, no doubt ashamed of himself for having asked her out. She couldn't imagine how much he was hurting now that he could no longer play hockey. Then he'd lost his wife to another man.

The icing on the cake would be for the media to report that he'd fallen low enough to be seen with a nobody who could barely fill a B cup.

And yet he didn't seem as if he regretted his choice of date for the evening. He acted genuinely interested in her and so like the man she'd thought he was at the rink that she relaxed and found herself telling him about some of her adventures in the classroom. Michael had always been bored and dismissive of her job. But Jarrad laughed at her stories, and regaled her with a few stories about him and his siblings as kids.

When he talked about the past, she could see him as a little boy. The image filled her with warmth.

He talked a lot with his hands, she noticed. They were big hands, the kind that wielded a hockey stick the way a Viking might have wielded a sword.

Twice she became completely distracted watching those big hands, imagining them on her body.

She grabbed her water and drank quickly, wondering if the wonderful wine he'd chosen had completely gone to her head. Or her nether regions. It was so unlike her to be having sexy thoughts about a stranger. And yet he wasn't a stranger. He seemed familiar to her somehow, and so easy to talk to.

Stranger or not, as the evening progressed, she realized she wanted him in the most elemental way. Even though they talked about a variety of subjects, not one of which was sexual, she knew, every time their gazes connected, that he was thinking the same thoughts. Suspected he knew she was too.

But she wouldn't go down that road again. If Michael had been too far above her on the social/sexual scale, this guy was in the stratosphere.

Michael's betrayal had hurt. Somehow, she thought that Jarrad's would devastate her.

"Your wrists are so tiny," he said, looking at her right hand toying with the bottom of her wineglass. It was the first really personal thing he'd said. He reached over, picked up her hand. At the touch of his tough, leathery fingers on her skin, she shivered. He wrapped his hand around her wrist and it was thicker than a gauntlet. "You make me feel like an oversized baboon." He glanced over at her, all steamy and delicious, "I'd be scared to break you."

She held his gaze. "I'm tougher than I look," she said. Then almost gasped at her own boldness. Where had that come from?

There was a beat of potent silence. He broke it, saying huskily, "I really want to kiss you right now."

Her heart jumped in her chest. The idea both panicked and excited her. She licked her lips.

And the way he gazed at them, she realized he'd mistaken her nervous gesture for a provocative one. Oh, crap. She was in so much trouble.

"Shall we go?" he asked.

She nodded.

As they left, he put a hand on her back, not exactly the most sexual gesture in history and yet she felt his heat burning through the material of her dress, felt the primal drumbeat of passion between them.

He walked her to his car, opened her door for her, and when he got into his own side, he didn't start the car right away. Instead, he leaned forward, closing the distance between them with tantalizing slowness. Then he captured her mouth with his, kissing her slowly as though savoring her.

Oh, he felt so good. She loved the shape of his mouth, the feel of his lips on hers, the rasp of stubble when his chin brushed her. He touched his tongue to her lips and she opened for him, greedy and wanting.

After about a year of kissing, he pulled away. Both of them were breathing fast. "I want to see you again."

"Mmm."

"Could it be tomorrow? I'm probably only going to be in town for a couple of weeks. I don't want to waste any time."

"A couple of weeks?" She felt chilled suddenly. This promising beginning already had its end?

And yet, on some level it was perfect. A brief fling with a great guy, somebody who couldn't hurt her because there wouldn't be time. He was the perfect antidote to the unpleasant aftertaste of Michael in her system. She hadn't even had a date since he'd humiliated her, she certainly hadn't kissed another man and she'd assumed it would be a long, long time before she'd trust a man enough to be intimate.

But then Jarrad had come along. Jarrad who was a celebrity, a wounded hero, a man so far above her he was more like a fantasy than an actual human being.

If he were permanently in Vancouver she couldn't put herself through the possibility of being crushed. But if he was only here for two weeks?

Then maybe he was absolutely, exactly perfect.

Besides, some demon had taken over her body, and she felt like a completely different woman with Jarrad.

If she only had two weeks, she didn't plan on wasting any of it.

She closed the distance between them, put her lips to his ear. "If we only have two weeks, why wait until tomorrow?"

He put a hand to the back of her neck, dipped her back so he could look at her face. "Are you saying what I think you're saying?"

She breathed in the scent of him. So uniquely his and so utterly seductive to her. "Yes."

5

HE DROVE BESIDE THE OCEAN, gray and moody as though depressed by the constant rain. He'd never realized how much he liked rain until he lived away from it. There was something comforting and familiar about the pound of raindrops on the roof, the splash of puddles in the road.

"Where are we going?" she asked once, as they headed over Lions Gate Bridge and into West Vancouver.

"My place."

"You keep a place here?"

"Sure. I bought it a while ago. I'm up here enough that it makes sense."

In fact, this had been his first real-estate purchase, the heady plunge of a guy who'd suddenly made it. Luckily, he'd had good advisors and enough people who'd smack him down in a second if he got too full of himself that they wouldn't let quick success go to his head.

But nobody could have talked him out of buying the house when he first saw it. Tucked away in a quiet cove on the waterfront, the house had originally been a summer cottage back before a bridge connected Vancouver with the north shore. Back when you had to take a ferry across.

Of course, since then waterfront property in West Van had risen in value with dizzying speed, and the home had been modernized, but it still had the bones of the original cottage and he'd resisted all ideas from well-meaning friends and his ex to knock the structure down and build a monster house. He didn't want a fancy mansion. He wanted privacy, an ocean view and a bit of beach. And a house that felt like home. He'd spent enough nights out of town and in hotels that he'd really come to value having a home.

Somehow, the Malibu place had never really felt like home to him. It was a status symbol, he supposed, a little like his wife had been.

Sierra, he realized with a start, was like his West Van cottage. Modest on the outside but real and comfortable in the way his favorite things always were.

He drove down the winding road that led to his place and a feeling of utter contentment stole over him. He loved this place and bringing this woman to it felt right.

He pulled into the little wooden shed that was the one-car garage, killed the engine and led her out and down the path to his house.

It didn't show at its best on a damp spring evening and even the ocean seemed kind of sullen and not inclined to show off for his guest. But the lights shone across English Bay in the Point Grey homes and the waves lapping against the rocky beach played their usual haunting music.

"Oh, Jarrad," she said. "It's beautiful."

"I'll show you the best part first," he said, very much hoping her words confirmed her as the ocean lover he was.

He took her hand, so small and fine-boned that he immediately loosened his grip, he was so scared of hurting her, and walked around to the front, where a previous owner had built a deck almost as big as the house. Half of it was covered by a glass awning so you could sit out, as he often did, and watch the storms. He turned on the outside heater and together they looked over the sea. He heard her breathe in deeply. "I love it here," she said.

"So do I. It's a special place."

She shivered slightly and he stepped behind her, putting his arms around her, pulling her against him. She was trim and shapely. Not a hard body, by any means, but soft, womanly.

He held her like that for a while, his chin just resting on the top of her head, breathing in the scent of the ocean, and of her.

After a bit she turned and lifted her face in mute invitation. Which he took immediate advantage of, bending to kiss her. Her lips were warm and tasted sweet against the tang of rain-tinged salt air, and when he pulled her in closer, she slid her arms up around his neck, kissing him back with passion. He loved her contrasts, the shy schoolteacher one minute and the bold, sexy woman the next.

They kissed for a while until they were both panting louder than the ocean, and she wrapped one leg around him, rubbing the back of his calf with her high heel. The gesture was so spontaneous he wondered if she even realized she was doing it.

"Would you like the full tour?" he murmured.

"Oh, yes," she said against his mouth.

He took her hand and led her inside. He flipped on a light and as he tried to see the room through her eyes, wondered if he should have hired a decorator. But she smiled. "I would have imagined that your living room would be all big-screen TV and, I don't know, hockey trophies."

"TV's behind there," he said, pointing to the rustic cabinet he'd bought when he first got the place. Of course, the TV hidden behind the distressed wooden doors wasn't exactly puny and it was plasma, but he didn't bother to explain all that.

For the rest, he'd bought most of the furniture from the old couple who were selling the place. It was sturdy and to his uneducated eye he thought it all went with the place. He still thought so. The furniture was wooden-framed, a lot of it made by the previous owner out of driftwood, with all the upholstery in blues.

"It's so rustic, but real, you know?" she said.

"Yeah." Exactly what he'd always thought.

He showed her where the bathroom was and the kitchen, which really did need a reno, even though he kind of liked the scarred old Formica counters and light oak cupboards.

Then he pointed to the closed doors that were his office (even though he didn't do any work) and guest bedroom (even though he didn't have any guests).

He really didn't want to play tour guide any more. He wanted her in his bed. And badly.

With that thought in mind, he said, "And here's my bedroom." And he led her through the main room to his bedroom. He felt her hesitate on the threshold, her hand going suddenly rigid in his. She was so sweet, he couldn't help himself from turning to nibble on her lips, to kiss her until the rigidity left her body and the passionate woman was back in his arms.

He led her forward into the room and she pulled away from him to say, "Oh, how beautiful." She wasn't referring to the original artwork he'd bought at some charity auction, but to the floor-to-ceiling windows. He could watch the ocean from his bed all day and all night. It was probably the main reason he'd bought the place.

The bed and bedding were his only nod to true luxury. He figured with the beating his body had taken over the years, a great bed was a necessity. And if Egypt had been picked clean of cotton so he could enjoy bedding that had cost more than his first car, then he was sorry, but he definitely enjoyed the comfort.

He turned down the bed, then drew her forward. She was smiling, but he could sense her shyness. He had no idea what her background or her story was, but he knew quite suddenly that he had to treat her carefully. Take it slowly.

"You know what I thought about over dinner?" he asked, nibbling her lips, then kissing her thoroughly.

"What?"

"How pretty your neck is." He kissed her again. "Long and elegant, like a dancer's."

"My neck?"

She didn't sound like it was the greatest compliment of her life.

"Among other things." He ran a fingertip along her collarbone. "I probably need to get you out of these clothes to confirm how pretty everything else is."

She snorted. The most unladylike thing he'd ever seen or heard her do. "It's not all that exciting."

"You let me be the judge of that," he said, and then, because he couldn't resist, he pulled her in and started kissing her again.

He thought he could kiss this woman all day and all night and never grow tired of it.

While they were mouth-to-mouth, he slipped his hands under the hem of her dress, raising it and reaching under. Her skin was warm and soft and as he touched her she made soft little sounds in her throat, like unspoken words of encouragement. He felt his blood start to heat as his hands trailed up to the edges of surprisingly sexy panties.

He'd planned to go so slowly, take it easy, but he sensed a heat coming off this woman, and a need that he felt in his caveman's heart. Abandoning caution, finesse, he turned her so her back was to him, dragged down the zipper, exposing her back and the lacy strap of a black bra. And her long, beautiful neck.

He kissed his way down, from bump to bump of her spine. He could feel her excitement, feel her moving against him as he followed the zipper's path with his lips, breaking contact between his mouth and her skin only long enough to slip the dress off her shoulders and let it drift to the floor.

He turned her around, took her mouth again. She still wore those crazy green-and-black shoes, and nothing else but a lacy black bra and panties. He had her bra unsnapped and sailing into the corner of the room in seconds, and then he pulled back to look at her.

"You are beautiful," he said, meaning it with every fiber of his being.

"No, I'm not," she sighed. "I'm so ordinary."

There was such sadness in the words, but how could she even think that about herself? Her neck was long, her shoulders elegant and her breasts high and firm. Her belly was slender, but slightly rounded as a woman's should be. Her stomach didn't sport a six-pack, but then he'd never thought a woman's belly should be indistinguishable from a guy's, not that he'd ever said that aloud.

She reached for his shirt and he helped her pull it off, then pulled her close again, enjoying the rub of her skin against his. "Am I too hairy for you?" He felt like an animal with a pelt, but she buried her face against his chest, licked his nipples.

"I love it," she said.

He pushed her back on the bed, toppling her so she fell laughing onto the mattress. He traced the waistband of her panties then dipped inside for a tantalizing touch of her soft sweetness.

All he did was touch her and she gasped, her back rising off the bed. And it was as if a bomb went off inside him. He needed to touch her, lick her, take her. He wanted to take her every possible way he could think of and maybe they'd invent a few new ones.

He was panting, already wanting to pound himself inside her body when he hadn't even begun to pleasure her yet. *Steady, boy,* he warned himself. He tried to remember that he'd planned to take this slowly, but then he hadn't known that Sierra would be so unbelievably responsive, or that her eyes would half close and she'd look at him the way Cleopatra must have looked at Anthony. Or that her skin would smell like honey and taste like rain-washed waves.

She was, in a word, gorgeous. And real.

He stripped her panties off because he simply had to see her, taste her.

While he was at it he stripped the rest of his clothes off too so they were both naked.

When he joined her on the bed, he could see her eyeing him, her eyes big and trusting and sparkling with excitement.

She reached over, ran her hands over his hairy chest, then down over his belly. Her hand was so small and yet so sensuous when she touched him. Before he'd even realized her intention, she'd closed her hand around him. He felt the slight quiver in her fingers, excitement or nerves, he had no idea, but it was like a hot, vibrating glove and he knew that if she clutched him like that for much longer he'd embarrass himself.

So he flipped himself on top of her, kissed his way down her body until she was squirming, then he pushed her legs apart and put his mouth on her. Right there. Right where she was so hot and honey-sweet.

She cried out when he licked her, and once he got her going, he practically had to hold onto her hips to keep her earthbound.

When he pushed his tongue all the way up inside her, she grabbed his head, clutching his hair with her fingers and pretty much screaming as her orgasm shook her. Her inner walls spilled honey on his tongue and pulsed around him as the aftershocks shook her.

SHE. COULD. NOT. BELIEVE. What. Had. Just. Happened. To. Her.

Each thought word was more like a pant.

Oh, oh. Oh. He was so good. It was all she could think. He was soo good. Naturally, he'd had decades of practice with supermodels, but right now she didn't care. It was as though he'd been designed with no other purpose than to give her pleasure.

He was kissing his way back up her body and her skin

was so supersensitized that she experienced little shocks of pleasure everywhere his tongue touched her.

When he got up close enough to kiss her, she tasted her own pleasure, and wondered how she'd ever got so lucky as to find herself in this amazing man's bed.

Sierra had never thought of herself as a tiger in bed. *Hah.* More like a stuffed animal when she'd been with Michael. Now, tonight, she wanted it all. She wanted to try everything she'd ever dreamed of, every passionate, crazy, fantasy she'd ever imagined.

Jarrad had probably done it all a thousand times, but she didn't care. She couldn't imagine a man more fun to try things with.

His hands were all over her. Jarrad touched her as though he loved the feel of her. As though she were the most amazing woman in history.

When he'd kissed her mouth for so long she was light-headed, he moved south. Kissing her chin, her throat and her chest. He spent a long time on her breasts, kissing and sucking them.

She tried to hold on to sanity long enough to remind him of the importance of protection, but he was already reaching for the night table and she relaxed, knowing that he might take chances on the ice, but he wouldn't take chances with her.

The sound of the tearing condom wrapper reminded her that she hadn't anticipated sex in a long time. Hadn't wanted a man inside her as much as she wanted this one in longer than she could remember. Maybe ever.

In a second he was ready, and she opened for him as he pushed slowly inside her.

The long, slow friction was heaven. And hell. She wanted him inside her so badly, even as she realized he was a big man, and holding himself back so as not to hurt her. But she was so hot, so needy, that she couldn't wait. She pulled him into her even as she thrust up against him.

"Oh, honey, you feel so good," he groaned. Oh, he had no idea how good she felt. Her body was melting from the inside out, and the more he thrust into her, the more she wanted.

She was mindless, crazed, and he soon caught her mood and joined in, not taking it easy but giving her everything he had.

She cried out, she was exploding, gripping and grabbing at him as they surged and bucked against each other, hard and strong and needy.

With a helpless groan, he followed her, stretching the incredible sensations out with a few long, slow strokes that left him shuddering until he fell limply on top of her.

A drop of sweat splashed onto her breast. "Oh, baby," he said. He turned onto his back, pulling her with him, she snuggled against him, loving the tickly feeling of his hairy chest against her cheek and the sound of his heart pounding beneath her ear.

When they'd both calmed a little, she said, "I saw your commercial tonight on TV."

He grimaced. "My condolences. I'm no Robert DeNiro."

"No. But you are the kind of man who is so famous he can move shaving cream."

He didn't seem to get her point. "They called it Ice. Can you imagine anything more lame?"

"Jarrad, you're a celebrity."

It was a moment before he answered, and what he said was, "I'm a washed-up hockey player."

Wow. She'd been so caught up with her own insecurities

she hadn't even thought about what it must be like for him, to have risen so high and now be retired before he was ready.

She rose on one elbow. "You are not a washed-up anything," she informed him. "Right now you are a hockey coach. Who knows what you'll end up being?"

"That's easy for you to say. Your work has meaning. Every morning when you wake up, you know you're changing lives. You are helping kids learn stuff and grow up to be good citizens. That is so much more important than shooting a puck down the ice."

She started to laugh. First a low chuckle that she tried to smother, then a snort emerged and finally she could hold it back no longer. She let out a huge howl of laughter.

"You are laughing? At my loss of career?"

"No. I'm laughing because I was so demoralized when I found out who you were that I would have canceled our date if I'd had your number."

"You're kidding, right?"

She shook her head. "No."

He rolled over, pinned her. "I am so glad you didn't have my phone number. Look what I would have missed."

She didn't even want to think about what she'd have missed.

"It's just that, you're, like, some celebrity that I'd see on TV and think, 'Wow, he's cute,' but not someone I'd ever meet in real life. I want to know what the real man is like."

"Okay. Ask me anything."

"Anything?"

"Yep."

"Promise to answer honestly?"

He narrowed his eyes at her. "If you promise not to

share anything I might tell you with anyone else. Especially anyone who might, say, carry a camera and a notebook and snoop on people for a living."

"Promise."

Now that she had his word he'd tell her anything, she had no idea what she wanted to ask him. She gazed up into those gorgeous green eyes and wondered if anything ever dented his armor. And there it was. Her question.

"When's the last time you cried?"

He sucked in a breath. "You don't want to start with an easy one? Like my astrology sign?"

"Nope."

Besides, all the easy stuff was on the internet. He was a Taurus, she already knew that. His sign was the bull, which seemed perfect.

He flopped on his back and stared at the ceiling, but kept a hand resting on her thigh so she still felt connected to him, warmed by his touch.

"When my father died," he finally said.

Her sympathy was immediately aroused. "I'm so sorry."

"It was so sudden. He was alive and joking last time I saw him, and then boom. He had a massive heart attack and he was gone." His voice thickened. "I never got to say goodbye. Never got to thank him for teaching me to skate."

A tear rolled down the side of his face and she felt her own eyes fill.

"Never got to tell him I loved him."

She kissed him. "He knew," she said softly. "He knew."

For a moment they lay there, her head on his shoulder and his arm wrapped around her. And for her, he wasn't a shaving-cream-commercial celebrity or a former NHL heavyweight, he was a man who missed his father. And who could open his heart to a woman.

"So," he said after a while. "Are we going to lie around blubbering or are we going for round two?"

Her body sparked immediately in response. "I pick round two."

"That's my girl." And he rolled over and kissed her. And let his hands roam all over her as though he couldn't ever get enough.

"Is there anything in particular I can do for you?" he asked in a low, sexy voice.

"Yes."

"What's that?"

She smiled the smile of a woman who is with a great lover.

"Everything."

6

SIERRA WOKE UP WITH A START, barely aware of what had woken her until she felt the unmistakable sensation of a man's lips on the back of her neck. She smiled, half in and half out of sleep, feeling the delicious sense of a body well-loved.

When his hands reached around to play with her breasts she realized she was naked. And that she'd fallen asleep.

"I fell asleep," she said, turning to face him. "I didn't mean to. I should probably get going."

His eyes were slumberous and sexy. "You should stay for breakfast," he mumbled. Now that the back of her neck was unavailable, he kissed his way across her shoulder, heading for her breast.

"Breakfast? I can't stay the whole night."

He stopped in his tracks and glanced up at her. "Darling, you already did."

Only now did she realize that it was light outside. She squinted at the fancy clock on the bedside. It was eight in the morning.

A strangled sound came out of her mouth. "I can't stay the night."

Amusement faded from his eyes and for a second she got a glimpse of the tough player who'd once terrorized opposing teams. "Why not? Somebody waiting for you at home?"

"What?" She rubbed her eyes, and, as his meaning sank in, she snapped, "No, of course not."

"Then what's the problem?"

"I don't—" She stopped, not sure how to explain her confused feelings, threw her hands up. "I just don't. Not any of it."

He still regarded her somewhat warily, but the sharp suspicion had faded. "Well, you sure did last night."

"It was different last night. It was dark and I thought it would be simple to slip into bed with a stranger and then slip out again and go home."

He stroked the side of her face with his finger, this tough guy with his delicate caresses. "But you're not built that way. I could have told you that."

"How could you know?"

He shrugged. "Gut instinct. A lot of women are interested in guys who play hockey. You get a sense of who wants bragging rights and who wants something real." A sudden frown darkened his eyes. "At least, most of the time you do. Sometimes we all get fooled."

She suspected he was thinking of the ex Mrs. Jarrad McBride and she really didn't want the shadow of a swimsuit model darkening this bed, especially not while she happened to be in it. Naked.

"I didn't even know who you were until I saw that commercial. Then I had to look you up on Google."

"I know." He stroked the side of her waist where it curved, traced it to her hip and let his hand settle there, warm and comforting.

"You must have thought I was stupid."

"Nope. I thought how nice it was to have a conversation with someone where I was just a guy she was getting to know."

"I can't believe how well I got to know you." She shook her head. "This time yesterday, I didn't even know you existed."

"Now you do."

She rolled over to face him. "I guess you're right," she agreed. "I'm not really the casual-sex type."

He kissed her nose. "Believe it or not, neither am I. I tell you what. Since I accidentally made you stay all night, how about I take you for breakfast?"

"How does that make me staying over here any better? If we go for breakfast?"

"Doesn't. But I'm hungry. I can't think when I'm hungry."

"Well…" But it wasn't like she had anything pressing to do at home. Laundry that could wait. And besides, after all their night-time activity, she was hungry too.

"Okay. But I need to shower first."

"Mind if I join you?"

"Jarrad."

"What?" He threw up his hands all Mr. Innocent. "It's a great way to save water. I'm all about saving the environment."

Because he was adorable and made her feel so good, how could she resist?

HE MIGHT HAVE TAKEN her to a fancy place for dinner but she discovered his taste in breakfast was more of the diner variety. Naturally, everyone knew him in Tracy's, where the choices for breakfast were pretty much bacon, eggs, sausage, pancakes and steak and eggs. This wasn't a place that would serve, say, muesli and yogurt, or an organic fruit compote.

Oh, well. She supposed a good dose of cholesterol wouldn't hurt her once in a while.

The coffee was good and strong, and while Jarrad launched into the West Coast Trucker which pretty much seemed to contain every single item on the menu times three, she stuck to bacon and eggs. Jarrad waded through all of his and still managed to eat half her hash browns.

"I don't know where you put all that food," she said, amazed.

"Sex," he said around a mouthful of potato. "It's fuel for sex."

She did not know how he did it, but even the stupidest comments like that one made her hot. She knew she only had him for a couple of weeks so she was determined to enjoy every minute.

Simply being here eating breakfast in a diner while wearing her black dress from last night made her feel gloriously wanton. She might as well wear a neon sign that said, Got Laid Last Night. Not that anybody spared her a second glance, but it was cool nonetheless.

She tried to cross her legs and felt a muscle twinge. "Ow."

"What's the matter?" he asked immediately. "Did I hurt you?"

"I don't think it was you. I think it was the hockey."

He seemed enormously relieved that it was hockey and not the aftermath of his loving making her wince. "You need to practice every day. Then your body will get used to skating and you'll get better fast."

"Jarrad, I have a job. I can't practice every day."

"Sure you can. When does your team meet up again?"

"Thursday."

"Okay. Come on. I'll give you a private coaching lesson today. We'll see if we can get you caught up enough that you can go after a puck without clinging to the boards."

"I need to change my clothes. I can't go skating in a little black dress."

He leaned forward. "I'm telling you right now that your thoughts are way too limiting. Haven't you ever watched figure skaters? They skate in dresses all the time." Then his voice lowered and he got that sexy look in his eyes that made her melt. "Imagine how it would feel, the cool breeze rising up underneath your skirt, maybe letting me get a little feel in if you manage to skate in a straight line without looking at your feet."

She tried to look prim and annoyed but only ended up laughing. "You are a sex maniac."

"Only with you."

She drank the last of her coffee. "Don't you have to coach the fire and police team today?"

"Hell." He smacked himself upside the head. "I totally forgot."

"That's okay." She wouldn't be disappointed. Sure, if she hadn't stupidly reminded him of his coaching gig, she'd be getting another private lesson, but she wasn't nearly as interested in skating as she was in some other physical activities they could do together.

However, she had reminded him, and of course that was the right thing to do. Now she had fewer than thirteen days with him. She had a feeling it was going to fly by.

"Can I call you later?"

Okay, so lucky thirteen was still a possibility. She nodded. Gave her best attempt at a seductive smile. "You can definitely call me later."

She must have done an okay job because he made a low

animal growl that called up a corresponding response in her body. Oh, yes, she'd be waiting by the phone.

BUT WHEN HE CALLED, it was with the disappointing news that he'd been delayed. "My brother and sister demanded a family dinner. We haven't all been together for a while. I didn't know how to get out of it. If I told them I had a date, then they'd ask a bunch of nosy questions about you, which I don't think either of us want."

"Right. Of course. I understand." And she did, all too well. She was his little secret. Not even his family could know about her. It was Michael all over again. Except that with Jarrad the sex was really good, and since she already knew he could never be hers for more than a couple of weeks, she wasn't hurt that he didn't want to own up to her presence in his life. At least, not very hurt.

Later, she was pretty sure she'd suffer when he was gone from her life, but in the meantime, it was so nice to be with him.

"Can I come over later? After dinner?" he asked.

"Oh, um…" It wasn't as if she had anything else to do to make a visit from a celebrity hockey player unwelcome. "Sure."

"Great. See you around ten."

Her apartment was neat. It was always neat, but with a gentleman caller coming later, she changed the sheets, vacuumed her bedroom, went out and bought fresh flowers. Then she ironed her best silk nightgown. The softness of the fine fabric and the thought that it would soon be the only thing separating her and Jarrad made her feel hot and twitchy.

She'd already enjoyed the best night of her life, how could she be so greedy as to be panting for a repeat? She'd never thought of herself as a particularly sexual woman.

Until now.

When she recalled how bold she'd been last night she felt her cheeks heat. But Jarrad had seemed to like it, and in truth, she'd liked that version of herself too. A woman who wasn't afraid to ask for what she wanted. To offer herself to a man who interested her.

She was strong, sexy, in control. She was right up there with Madonna.

Though she doubted the Material Girl ironed her own nightgowns—if she even wore them—or spent an afternoon correcting the spelling of second graders.

She decided to continue on her road to personal boldness and while she was waiting for Jarrad, did her hair in sexy curls, slipped on her silk nightgown and imagined meeting him at the door wearing so little that she was a blatant invitation.

Then he was there, buzzing her to get in. "Come on up," she said, and then panicked. What was he going to think of her? Her outfit pretty much begged for sex. Maybe he was here to talk about coaching, to get some more of her advice for seven-year-old boys.

She raced into her bedroom, tore off the gown, shoved herself into jeans and a sweater, and ran to get the door when he knocked.

She opened the door.

He stepped inside.

She was in his arms.

He kissed her for a long, long time. "I've been thinking about this all day," he told her.

"Me, too." And then she cursed herself for being such a chicken. She should never have changed. On the other hand, now she'd have the pleasure of having him undress her.

He backed her into the living room, still kissing her.

Oh, it was nice to be in the arms of someone so athletically coordinated. By the time they got to the couch, she was panting with desire.

So was he.

She wondered why she'd bothered changing her sheets. They never made it to the bedroom.

Much later, when they were sprawled on the couch talking idly, he said, "So, did you practice today?"

"No. I had marking to do."

"It's very important to practice."

"I can do it when you're there, but when I'm on my own I kind of freak out."

"Well, until you get the hang of it, I guess I'll need to be there with you," he said, perfectly cheerfully. As though teaching a complete novice how to play hockey was as much fun as playing in the NHL.

"Really? You'd do that?"

"Sure." He stretched his arms over his head. She could have watched him do that for hours. The muscles in his arms were so sexy, so defined. His chest was broad, his belly a classic six-pack. She felt like drooling every time she looked at him. "You tired?"

She didn't think she'd ever be too tired for more sex with this amazing man. "No." She glanced up at him from under her lashes. "What did you have in mind?"

"Hockey, of course," he said, with a wide "gotcha" grin. He leaped up and pulled her to her feet. "Come on."

"You can't be serious."

"I never joke about the world's greatest game."

"But it's after midnight."

"I know."

"We'll never get in the rink."

He began pulling on his clothes. Glanced up at her. "Care to make a small wager on my chances?"

In that moment she saw the little boy in him, the hockey hellion he must have been as a kid. Charm and talent and guts. What a combination.

"I think I'll save my money for something sensible. Like bail for when we get thrown in jail for breaking and entering."

"Put your clothes on and stop stalling, woman."

She couldn't imagine Michael ever calling her "woman." He was much too politically correct. But the strange thing was that Michael had all the veneer of a man who respected women, while Jarrad might talk like a redneck, but he was the one willing to teach a hapless female how to play hockey. Actions, she reminded herself, speak louder than words.

"Yes, sir," she said and put her clothes back on.

"I like your hair like that, by the way," he said.

"Thanks."

"Now go get your stuff."

7

OF COURSE SHE'D KNOWN he'd get into the rink. But it was even easier than she'd imagined.

"Big J!" The night manager had been thrilled to welcome them into the complex in the middle of the night.

And he talked all the way as he led them to a rink. Mostly about Jarrad's team and some of the game highlights he recalled.

"It's a damn shame, what happened to you," he said at last.

"Ah, I had a good run. I'd have had to retire soon anyway. Not getting any younger."

He talked a good line, but she suspected he wasn't having an easy time adjusting to his unexpected retirement. The man had too much energy. Well, witness him bringing her here at midnight to skate. After sex.

The lights were dim, and it was sort of spooky seeing all the ghostly trophies in cases and feeling the emptiness of the usually bustling space.

The night manager unlocked the rink and hit the lights. "You've got the whole place to yourselves," he announced cheerfully.

"Now, doesn't that sound good?"

Everything with him sounded good.

She couldn't believe how much fun it was. He teased her, bullied her, pushed her, and by the end of two hours, she pretty much forgot she wasn't back playing field hockey. Skating was beginning to feel natural again, she'd lost her fear and concentrated on getting the puck—which seemed to fly around at astonishing speeds across the ice—and smacking it in the general direction of the other goal.

"Okay, champ," he said, skating up and giving her a hug. "You can hit the showers now."

"Hit the showers?" she said, laughing. "I guess I'll have to wait until I get home."

But a teasing, sexy smile was already squinching up his eyes, and that one extra-long scar-turned-laugh-line pulled her in. "I say we shower here."

"At two in the morning?"

"Who cares what time it is, we're sweaty and I am personally very, very dirty."

She laughed so suddenly the sound echoed around the empty rink. "You certainly are." She shrugged. Since she'd become involved with Jarrad she knew nothing was ever going to be normal and staid. "Okay, I'm not sure where the women's change room is."

His wicked grin only intensified. "I bet you've always wanted to see where the naked men shower."

Not until now. But the very words had her conjuring him up naked and soapy and her naked and soapy and… "You read my mind," she said, her voice going low and sexy in spite of herself.

He chuckled, deep in his throat. Grabbed her hand. "Come on."

A deep ache began low in her belly. There was something about this man that made the craziest things deeply erotic.

They walked down the dim, empty corridor to the men's shower. He entered first, hit the lights.

"You know, this isn't the most erotic place I've ever been," she said, regarding the harshly lit shower room. Wooden benches, metal lockers, a row of sinks and mirrors and big shower cubicles weren't exactly equivalent to a spa. Still, it was ruthlessly clean. And he was here with her.

"It gets better when you're naked," he promised her.

And then he pulled her to him and began to kiss her. And like that she zoomed from zero to a hundred.

She was running on an adrenaline high from the fun of skating in the middle of the night, and she was tired too, which added to the surreal feeling. She caught a glimpse of herself in one of the mirrors and barely recognized her usually neat self. Her hair was a mess, her cheeks were flushed from exercise, cold and probably lust, and her lips were puffy and wet from his kisses.

She was so happy her school was closed that Monday, stretching out an amazing weekend.

Her clothes felt suddenly too heavy, enormous, like a ski suit in summer. She began pulling off clothing, grabbing it, dragging at it, not remotely caring that the night manager could walk in at any time.

Jarrad caught her fever—or maybe she'd caught it from him—and yanked and pulled at his own clothing until there was nothing but a pile of discarded fabric between them.

He was the most glorious thing she'd ever seen naked. And the way his eyes worshipped her, she knew he liked her more modest body too. Which made her feel beautiful.

He started the shower and then pulled her in under the flow of water. She sputtered a little as her head went straight under, then pulled out and enjoyed the sluice of wetness over her hot, sweaty skin.

Big hands reached for her, soaped up and ready. The light was ridiculous, fluorescent, bouncing off white tile. She'd been in five-star hotel bedrooms that weren't as exciting.

He soaped her breasts, thoroughly, kissing her with his wet mouth. And as his hands began to roam, cleaning her thoroughly, she felt herself begin to dissolve.

"Turn around." His voice was low and commanding in her ear.

She did. Felt his hands, rough and tender, move over her back, her hips, rubbing her butt, her thighs.

"Spread your legs." Again the commanding tone, which she kind of liked. She thought about refusing, to see what he'd do, but she so wanted him there that she complied, easing them apart a little bit.

"More."

A spurt of lust shot through her. She spread. Wider.

And he touched her with fingers that were exquisitely sensitive on those big, rough hands. Her hands grasped the white, shiny tile, as slick with wetness as she was herself, she felt she needed something to hang on to or she'd slide in a boneless heap at his feet.

While he rubbed her, she felt his cock, hard and eager at her back, bumping her gently as she moved helplessly against his magic fingers.

Heat built and she heard herself moan, resting her cheek against the cool tile. Closing her eyes against the bright light, while the water pounded down over them.

Climax flowed through her, sudden and pure, like the streams of water coming down. She turned, half blind with passion and water, reached for him. "My turn," she said and took the soap.

Soaping up his chest was a delight. She loved the hairiness of him, the big lather she created and then rubbed all over him. Over his gorgeous athlete's biceps, his ropy forearms and wrists, his hands, finger by finger, while she made other parts of him wait.

He'd commanded her and she'd obeyed. Would he be as smart?

"Turn around," she ordered in imitation of the way he'd spoken to her.

She thought he raised an eyebrow, but it was hard to tell with all the steam and water. He turned.

She smiled to herself, enjoying having her hands on his lovely, muscular back. His butt was round and hard. She washed all the way down his legs, and then without words, turned him, so his jutting cock was level with her mouth.

When he saw her intent, he said, "Oh, baby, yes."

She opened for him, took him in. Loved him with her mouth.

He was so beautiful, so hard and deliciously big. She explored all of him with her tongue, licking underneath, taking his balls gently in her mouth which made him shudder and moan.

He was hers completely. She loved the heady sense of her own female power. Playing with him, torturing him just a little as she built him up slowly, keeping control so he had to adjust to her pace.

"You are killing me," he groaned, and then she took pity on him and let him fly.

He pulled her to her feet, kissing her deeply.

"You are everything," he said.

8

ON THEIR WAY OUT, Jarrad stopped to thank the night manager for letting them in. He noticed that Sierra hung back, as though the guy would know what they'd been doing. Which, come to think of it, he probably did.

Jarrad felt like he had when he'd first been drafted. As though everything was ahead of him and he could do anything he put his mind to.

He stopped dead, astonished to find that the darkness which had plagued him since he first found out he wouldn't be playing professionally anymore had mysteriously lifted.

How could one school-teaching, fledgling hockey-playing, sweetheart of a woman change a man in such a short time?

It couldn't be possible.

But if not, then how else to explain the sudden knowledge that everything was going to be all right?

He turned to leave and the guy said, "Oh, by the way, we had some press types here earlier lookin' for you."

Irritation tried to poke holes in his feeling of happiness. "What did you tell them?"

"Told 'em to piss off," then he nodded to Sierra. "If you'll pardon the expression."

"Certainly," she said, always polite.

"Thanks," Jarrad said and grabbing her hand they left.

Even though it was 3:00 a.m. or so, he still checked the parking lot before hustling the pair of them into his car.

As they hit the road, he said, "I guess I figured they wouldn't bother me up here. So my ex is hooking up again, so what?"

She touched his hand with hers, and he felt ridiculously reassured. "I'm sorry."

"What are you sorry about? I'm the one dragging you into a mess no woman needs. I'm sure you don't want your students asking what you're doing hanging out with that guy who used to play hockey. Or your girlfriends and family asking a bunch of questions you might not be ready for."

Her hand gripped his so suddenly he was startled. "Is that why you've been hiding me?" He turned and found her eyes big and serious as she regarded him.

"I haven't been hiding you. I've been trying to protect you."

"I thought—I thought— Oh, never mind." She shook her head and turned forward once more.

"You thought what?"

"I thought I wasn't important enough for you. Not high-profile enough I guess. Not a celebrity."

"You have got to be kidding me."

She shook her head, kind of sadly. "I'd love the world to see us together. I want to meet your family. But then, with only two weeks, I figured we'd keep it quiet, then no one has to know."

"What do you mean two weeks?"

"Before you go back."

Had he really said that? He put an arm out and pulled her to him. "You know what's great about being retired? You can do anything you want with your time. I don't have to go anywhere."

She turned back to him and he thought her face was the most beautiful sight in the world.

"We've only started this thing. Who knows where it will lead? All I know is that you make me feel like the world's full of possibilities again. I think I lost that after the accident."

He looked at her for a long moment before continuing. "You're smart and sexy and beautiful and you care about people."

"I'm a teacher, not a fancy celebrity."

"Exactly. You're a great teacher. You're teaching me to live again and to quit coasting along making dumb-ass commercials for something to do. Maybe I'll coach, maybe I'll build stuff."

"Build stuff?"

"Sure. I used to love working with my hands. I built furniture and all kinds of things when I was younger. Then hockey took over my life. I don't need more money. I need something to do. I guess I got so caught up in who I used to be that I forgot there's a whole new life out there waiting for me."

"Of course there is." She spoke with so much confidence in him, how could she understand what that meant? He didn't want to scare her since they'd only begun, but he had a pretty strong feeling that Sierra was going to be a part of that future.

He caught a dream image glimpse of the two of them in the future. He bet she wouldn't let him build a crib because of some safety thing, but he was bound and determined to build a high chair. That he could do.

And maybe a rocking horse.

He'd have go dig up his dad's old tools and start practicing.

The contentment was like a warm blanket around his heart. "Anything you need to go home for?"

She shook her head. "School's closed tomorrow. I threw a few extra things in my sports bag, in case I got an invitation I couldn't refuse."

"That's my girl."

NEXT MORNING, HE WOKE up feeling better than he'd felt in a long time. With a jolt, he realized he was alone in bed. Surely she hadn't gone squirrely on him and snuck off home?

Then he heard the greatest sound in the world, next to those panting cries she made when she came. He heard the sound of a woman singing in the kitchen.

In his experience, a woman singing in the kitchen this early meant she was making something like coffee. Or breakfast in bed.

Sure enough, she waltzed in a few minutes later, wearing one of his T-shirts that dropped almost to her knees, looking sexy as hell and bearing a tray. Okay, so it was healthier stuff than he usually ate, and maybe the portions were a little skimpy, but he didn't feel like complaining.

After breakfast, they sat around drinking coffee and reading the paper, then after a nice round of midmorning sex followed by a shower, he said, "Let's go meet my family."

"Are you sure? I didn't mean right away."

"I don't know what that ex of yours did to you, but since you've helped me get over my little problem of feeling sorry for myself, I figure it's the least I can do to return the favor and demonstrate how much I want to show you off."

She nibbled her lip. "I don't know what to wear. What if your family doesn't like me? What if—"

He stopped her feeble protests with his lips. "Do you know what they called my ex-wife?"

She shook her head.

"Gold Digger Barbie."

"Ouch," she said, but he could tell she was pleased. "I'm not a gold digger."

"I know. You're a teacher."

She grinned at him. "Right."

"Also a real, intelligent woman. They are going to fall down and kiss your feet."

She giggled. "Okay."

"Dinner tonight?"

"Sounds good."

"I'll give you a lift home, pick you up again later."

They drove out of his place and when he saw the car and the man at the top of his drive, he let out a string of curses that had Sierra's jaw dropping.

"Damn vipers," he said finally.

"Press?"

"Yeah. This one's a sports blogger. He's not the worst. But if he prints something, everybody will pick it up."

He made to roar by the guy, and then at the last minute changed his mind. He pulled over. Looked over at Sierra. "You sure about being okay if we're outed?"

Her eyes shone back at him, and he thought he'd do anything, anything at all to make sure this woman stayed in his life. "Sure."

"Okay, let's do it."

He got out of the car. Went around slowly to open

Sierra's door. Then, with his arm around her, he confronted the blogger. He hadn't realized there was another van parked half a block away. A TV crew. Who was he, Céline Dion, that the Canadian press should be so excited about his doings?

He heard the camera whir and tamped down his irritation. He knew that once they had their story they'd be on their way. The duller the story, the less intrusion he'd have in his life.

"Hey, guys. What can I do for you?" he asked, at his most benign.

"Just have a few questions for you, Big J," the blogger began.

"Shoot."

"How do you feel about your former wife getting engaged to Ogden Terry? The NBA superstar?"

"I wish her well. She's a great woman and he's a good guy. I hope they'll be very happy." To his immense surprise, he found that he actually meant those words. His marriage had been pretty much a disaster, since they'd both been such different people. He hadn't given her what she'd wanted any more than she had him. He genuinely hoped she'd find what she was looking for with the next guy.

"Really? She says you're an overgrown boy with emotional issues."

He smiled. "Well, I'm working on them."

"Who's this?"

"This is Sierra."

"She your new girlfriend?"

There was a beat of silence. The sun was making a valiant effort to peek out from behind the clouds, casting golden glints on the gray water. "Yes."

"Congratulations." The camera and all attention turned to Sierra. "Can you tell me how you two met?"

Her dimples peeped out. "At the skating rink."

They asked her what she did for a living, the spelling of her name, a few easy questions and then the zinger. The headline-grabbing, sound-bite-making, zinger.

"So, are you guys in love?"

She turned to him, wise and mischievous all at the same time. "We're working on it," she said, and then leaned in and kissed him while the camera whirred.

"Well?" she said when the media left. "How was that?"

"So much more satisfying than shooting a shaving commercial," he said.

"Come on, let's go back inside and get naked."

THEY WERE MORE LIKE GODS than people, Sierra thought when she first saw the three McBrides together. They were gathered at Jarrad's house for dinner and Jarrad was cooking. Well, he was supposed to be doing the cooking, but it seemed that the whole family had opinions on how to grill a steak on the barbecue.

All three McBrides were built on a larger scale than Sierra was used to. Not only were they physically imposing but all of them shared a kind of energy that drew your attention and held it.

Samantha, Jarrad's younger sister, the closest to him in age, greeted Sierra with friendliness, but there was suspicion in her gaze. The woman was gorgeous, with long, dark hair, striking features and a tall, athletic body that Sierra would kill for.

While she made Caesar salad, she grilled Sierra more thoroughly than Jarrad was grilling the steaks. Everything from her family to her job to her dating history was fair game. Finally, Jarrad said, "Hey, Sam, play nice. Sierra's not a hostile witness. She's my new girlfriend."

Samantha smashed garlic with gusto. "You have such appalling taste in women that I want to make sure she's for real."

Sierra and Jarrad exchanged glances. There was so much warmth in his gaze that she felt she'd melt if she looked at him too long. "Oh, she's for real all right," he said. "And the best thing that ever happened to me."

"I like her," Taylor said. Taylor was the youngest. He had so much restless energy that he never stayed still. But she'd liked him immediately. He had a frank way of looking at a person, and a smile that could thaw ice. "It's about time somebody in our family got serious. Mom's going to have a fit if we all stay single much longer."

"Ah, we only just started dating," Sierra pointed out. She was pretty sure she wanted to marry Jarrad, but not because his family pushed him into it.

"Sam?" Taylor said. There was a jokiness about the way he spoke. As a teacher she could usually spot a youngest. They were often the class clown.

"Don't look at me," Samantha said. "I like being single." She said it in a way that sounded like a challenge, and Sierra had to wonder what that was about.

"Well, I'm the baby of the family. I'm way too young to get married," Taylor said. "Gotta get to the NHL first. Then I'll hook up with a movie star."

"You are so full of it," Samantha said. Then she turned to Sierra. "It's a good thing you're an elementary school teacher. Hanging around with these two will remind you of your students."

Sierra smiled and sipped her wine. Yes, she thought, as they continued to squabble, Jarrad's family had definitely accepted her.

She glanced up to find Jarrad looking at her. *I love you,* he mouthed.

She smiled at him in a way that would let him know she'd show him exactly how much she loved him back.

Later.

In the Sin Bin

1

"CAN YOU NEVER ADMIT to being wrong?" Millicent Parker demanded of Samantha McBride.

Sam smiled the smile of a lawyer who knows she's about to settle out of court. "Not when I'm being paid a lot of money to be right."

Opposing counsel shook her head and unclipped her pen. "Okay. My client wants to stay out of court. He's given me a certain amount of leeway. Let's get this deal done. You're asking way too much for a wrongful dismissal suit and you know it. Your client's position was made redundant and he was given a fair exit package."

"He's fifty-nine years old and showing early signs of dementia. We both know that's why he was made redundant. He'll never find another job and *you* know it."

Millicent sighed. "All right, what's your bottom line?"

Sam settled her computer closer and did what she did best. Argued her position.

Samantha had been blessed—or cursed depending on how you looked at it—with no ability to see the so-called gray areas of an argument. Something was right or it was wrong. For her there was no middle ground. It made her a fierce lawyer, but sometimes in her personal life, her implacability caused a certain friction.

She'd be married by now if she had a different personality. For a second she allowed her thoughts to stray to the man she'd loved so long ago, but she'd become an expert at steering her mind away from painful thoughts of the past.

Back to business. Always business, where rules were clear and if there was any doubt, a judge would always decide. There were no gray areas, no "if onlys" in her practice, and that was exactly how she liked things.

She was feeling pretty damned pleased with herself when she got home from work later that day. As she was changing for her run, the phone rang. Normally, she didn't deviate from her routine, but when she saw it was her older brother calling, she grabbed the phone, one leg in her running tights.

"Hi, Jarrad. How's the coaching going?" If there was ever a good news/bad news scenario it had to be recently learning that her big brother was coming home to Vancouver where he belonged. That was the good news. Naturally, she'd assumed that he'd finally listened to her excellent arguments on the reasons for returning home and not wasting his life in Hollywood.

However, the bad news part of the equation was that he was here not because he'd heeded her superior advice, but because Greg Olsen had asked him to coach the amateur firefighters and police league. Greg Olsen. Of all people.

She'd wanted her big brother to come home and figure out what he wanted from life. He had a boatload of money and he'd enjoyed a decade of success in pro hockey. Now he could do anything. Go back to school, open a business, travel the world. Instead he'd informed her he was coming to coach.

"You're coaching? Seriously?" Sam could not believe her ears, and she'd heard some improbable stories in her seven years as a practicing lawyer. "Hockey?" she wanted to clarify to make sure she hadn't misunderstood. Perhaps her older brother had completely lost his mind and was coaching synchronized swimming or something. Though, based on his marriage to the swimsuit model, she doubted he wanted to get close to that many women in tank suits anytime soon.

"Yes. Hockey." Jarrad had sound vaguely irritated. "Of course, hockey."

And now, weeks into the coaching thing, he was calling her. "Can I come up?"

"You're here?"

"Right outside your building."

She rapidly considered her options. She could say no. Not an option with a big bro who had always been there for her and had so rarely asked for help. She could make him come running with her. Also probably not an option since he'd go at his athlete's pace and then she'd get competitive and run too fast for conversation.

So, she'd run later. She yanked her tights off. "Yeah, sure you can come up." And then she scrambled into a clean pair of jeans and a blue shirt.

When Jarrad arrived, he said, "I need your help."

"Trouble with Sierra?" She hoped that wasn't it. She really liked Sierra and to see Jarrad with a sweet, normal woman was like seeing him grow up. She didn't want to find out that he'd regressed again.

He waved her words aside. "Nothing, but Sierra doesn't understand hockey the way you do."

"I think we both need a beer to have this conversation,"

she said, crossing into her galley kitchen to the fridge and pulling out two cold Granville Island lagers. She didn't bother to offer him a glass, and, having grown up with brothers, she didn't take one herself. They twisted off the tops and both drank.

"So, is the problem hockey or Sierra?" She really needed clarification.

Her big brother looked at her as though she might have drunk twelve beers instead of taking one sip. "What are you talking about? I love Sierra. It's the coaching gig that's the problem."

She crowed with delight and launched herself at him. "I knew it. I knew she was the one." She squeezed her arms around his all-muscle middle. "This time it's real love, isn't it?"

A crooked smile dawned, "Yeah. The forever kind."

"Ooh, I can't wait to be an auntie."

"Sam, stop being a girl," he ordered her sternly. "We're talking hockey here."

"Right." She pulled out of his arms, but nothing could stop the happy feeling inside her. At least one of them looked as though they had a solid romantic future ahead of them. "So, hockey."

"Yeah. I'm coaching Greg's team."

"I know."

His long legs ate up the polished concrete floor of her Yaletown loft. Eight hundred and sixty two square feet had never felt so tiny. She was growing dizzy from watching him.

"You don't seem very happy about it." Sometimes, she'd discovered, stating the obvious was the best way to get people talking. This time was no different.

"Happy?" He swung round and actually stopped in his

tracks long enough to make eye contact. "How can I be happy about it?"

She thought about how it must feel to be an NHL heavyweight benched forever and the only coaching gig around was for a bunch of fire and police geezers. "Maybe this will be a stepping-stone to other coaching opportunities."

He shook his head at her, as though she'd said something incredibly dumb. Which couldn't be possible. "I don't know how to coach."

Ah, so it wasn't the humiliation of the team, but fear of his own shortcomings that was stopping him.

She walked forward, laid a hand on his shoulder. "How did you learn to play hockey?"

"You were there. You saw me."

"Only if I hung out at the rink. You were always at the rink."

"Yeah. Exactly. That's how I learned to play."

"Right. You practiced. Hour after hour. Maybe coaching is the same. You practice."

"I don't know. These guys are seriously messed up. It's so bad I'm taking advice from an elementary school teacher."

She bit back a smile. Coaching wasn't the only thing he was learning from Sierra Janssen.

"Here's the thing, Sam, you have a good eye. Remember when you figured out way back in high school that moving Tom Delaney from right wing to left would improve the team? And we moved him and it was amazing?"

"I remember. But it was easy to spot from the bench. He couldn't shoot left worth a damn. But if he shot right, he had a killer aim."

"Not everyone can spot those things. You've got an

instinct. And you know hockey so I don't have to explain anything."

"I don't know."

"Come on, you've been complaining since I got to town that we hardly see each other."

"I was referring to having dinner together or hanging out, not me helping you coach a bunch of over-the-hill amateurs."

"Look. Come down to the rink on Saturday morning. You've got good judgment, let me know what you think."

Her hand came off her brother's shoulder and clenched involuntarily at her side. "Is Greg going to be there?"

Jarrad's eyes narrowed in irritation. "Of course he's going to be there. He's on the team. Come on. You guys are ancient history. I'm sure you could be in the same hockey rink without killing each other."

She wasn't so sure about that.

Talk about complicated.

"I know you don't understand, but—"

"You're right. I don't. No one does. So, you guys went out all through high school, then you went away to college and you broke up. Big deal. Happens all the time."

"Well, there was a little more to it than that." She still experienced a weird ache in her chest at the thought of all the history that was between her and Greg Olsen. They hadn't only been boyfriend and girlfriend in high school. Looking back she realized now they'd been truly in love. They were probably the only two high-school sophomores who *got* Romeo and Juliet, who really deep-down understood the kind of teenaged passionate love that would cause you to die for each other rather than live alone.

And yet she'd killed that love more completely than Romeo and Juliet had perished.

In the most mundane manner. When Greg asked her to marry him, right before she'd left to go to law school in Toronto, she'd seen the gesture as an attempt to control her. As though he didn't trust her to stay faithful to him.

Oh, they'd seen each other in the intervening years since she'd been back in Vancouver. Ironically enough, usually at the wedding of an old friend from high school.

They were polite, like distant acquaintances, the kind where you recognize a face but can't recall the person's name. Before, he'd been the first person she thought of when she woke in the morning, the last one she talked to at night.

Jarrad was right. What was the big deal? Her brother was coaching the team. So what if her old boyfriend was part of the group? He was an old flame who'd sputtered out long ago.

"Sure," she said. "I'll swing by on Saturday."

Maybe it was time to make peace with the past.

2

THE MULTI-RINK COMPLEX housed everything from kids'
amateur teams to the Vancouver Canucks training. The
place was hopping on a Saturday morning. Even though
Samantha had given up precious sleep to be here at
7:00 a.m. she knew many of the players would have started
while it was still dark outside.

She passed a yawning pair of parents carrying coffee
in refillable containers that sported a kids' hockey-team
logo. Acquired in a team fundraiser no doubt.

Before entering the rink where Jarrad was coaching,
she stopped to fix her scarf in the neck of the absurdly expensive black woolen jacket she'd never even worn before.
Even as she'd cursed herself for doing it, she'd taken extra
time with her hair and makeup this morning, as though
she were preparing for an important day in court, not to
sit in on an amateur hockey practice at a ridiculously early
hour.

She slipped into the rink where the cops and firefighters
were practicing. There was Jarrad, one foot up on a bench,
watching as the men practiced a scoring drill. They were
passing the puck down the ice once, twice and then the
third guy shot for the net.

Twenty or so men skated around the rink, but only one drew her attention. The way he always had.

She moved closer, greeted Jarrad and passed him the takeout coffee she'd brought him.

"Thanks," he said absently, his eyes never leaving the rink.

Her gaze was fixed too, but on a more specific object. He looked so familiar and yet so new. The flop of dark hair she'd loved to play with was shorter now, but still thick and dark and her fingers itched to feel it. He'd grown into his face and it was harder, stronger than in his youth. His body had filled out, too. He wasn't the tallest guy on the team, but he was solid and commanding.

As though he felt her gaze on him, she saw Greg's head lift, and he scanned the benches. She wanted to glance away, not be caught staring at him, but somehow she was powerless to move her gaze until it connected with his and the impact was like a charge of electricity zapping her. For a long moment they stayed like that, gazes connecting, all the intimate past roaring back to her in a rush.

"Hey, Olsen. Wake up."

He turned his head, caught the puck and the practice continued. He didn't again glance her way. She knew because she never let him out of her sight.

Jarrad had clearly overcome his reticence about his coaching abilities. He hollered, hooted and occasionally walked onto the ice to explain a move in detail. Sometimes borrowing a player's stick to demonstrate. She knew he'd had a great career, but still she felt a pang for all he'd had to give up.

She'd intended to watch for a bit and then slip out, but, in spite of herself, she got pulled in. Enjoyed watching her brother explore skills she doubted he'd known he possessed.

Once she left the rink to fetch herself and Jarrad another coffee, otherwise she remained glued to the action. Fascinated.

"Well? What do you think?" he asked her at one point.

She thought he was an amazing coach and she felt so proud of him that she wanted to kiss him. But, of course, he was her big brother and she'd always shown her toughest side around him, so she said, "I think the young guy on defense should be up front. He's got great instincts and did you see the speed he put behind that puck?"

Her brother's brow crinkled in a frown. "I know. But he's a rookie on the force. The guys aren't going to want to see a rookie up front. It's like getting a private to lead a platoon."

"Is this a game of hockey or politics?"

He didn't say anything. But ten minutes later, he went down to the ice and tried a new formation, with the kid as center forward. She could feel the ripple of annoyance go through the team, but after they started practicing again, there was no doubt that their front line was stronger.

Jarrad was right, she thought, smiling to herself. She did have an instinct.

When at last the players were done for the day she rose, gathering her things, planning to leave before the guys came off the ice.

She was certain Greg would find a way to hang back, coming off the ice last, giving her time to vacate the premises. To her surprise, she'd barely made it five feet when that oh-so-familiar voice hailed her. "Hey, Sam, hold up."

The fact that Greg Olsen was calling her name was astonishing. That he'd obviously pushed his way off the ice first to do so was almost beyond belief.

She turned. He hadn't had time to remove his skates so he wobbled as he hiked up toward her. "What is it?" Not the most intelligent question, maybe, but all she could think of to say. He hadn't sought her out in years.

He was sweating, his dark hair plastered to his forehead. There was a shadow of stubble on his cheeks and chin. "I saw you sitting up there with Big J and thought it's been a while since we caught up. I know it's early, but what say I take you for a White Spot burger platter and a chocolate shake?"

In spite of herself she smiled. If he'd offered her coffee at a fancy coffee shop, cocktails at a funky bar on Granville Island she'd have said no. But the meal he outlined had been their favorite back when they'd been together. They'd plowed through a lot of burgers and downed a lot of chocolate shakes in their time as a couple.

Maybe it was the wash of memory, or the shock that he'd actually gone out of his way to speak to her, but even as her smart, rational brain was saying, *No, don't do it!* Her lizard brain was licking its dry little lips at the idea of sitting across from him at their old haunt once more.

"Okay."

A grin cracked his face. "Great. Give me fifteen minutes to shower. Be right back."

But the thought of hanging around waiting for him, having Jarrad and whoever else was still around see her and Greg leave the rink together was too much. She shook her head. "I'll meet you there."

He nodded once. Then turned and headed for the showers.

She had some emails and calls to catch up on. The wonder of modern technology meant she could do it from her iPhone in the parking lot of the restaurant.

It didn't seem like she'd done much of anything when a battered 4X4 drew up and Greg jumped out.

She stepped out of her car and greeted him with the casual familiarity of old friends. Except that her heart didn't usually trip so fast for old friends.

"Hungry?" he asked as he held the door open for her to pass into the restaurant.

"I haven't had a burger in forever."

"Then today is your lucky day."

As soon as they were settled into a booth, awkwardness descended. She opened the menu for something to do, then felt ridiculous since the whole point of coming here was to recreate their old ritual. And why she'd agreed, she couldn't imagine.

"They've got a lot of new menu choices," she said. "Lots of lighter, healthier fare."

"Yeah. And they still serve burgers and shakes. Because some things never change."

"Don't they?" she asked. Her gaze rose from the menu to connect with his. For a guy with a Swedish name he was very dark. She knew why, of course. His Swedish sailor grandfather had married a woman from the Squamish nation. Greg had always been ridiculously proud of his native blood. With his dark hair and eyes, high cheekbones and warrior's body, he'd been a good-looking boy. A dangerously good-looking, if skinny, teen and as a young adult he'd shown the promise of being a gorgeous man.

Now, at thirty-two, he'd fulfilled that promise. His body had filled out, and even if she hadn't known he was a cop she'd have guessed he worked out. There wasn't an ounce of fat on him. He looked fit, lean and dangerous.

Familiar and strange all at once.

"It was the craziest thing this morning. I looked over at you in the stands and I felt like I was back in high school, with my girlfriend there to cheer on the team." He grinned at her. "Even if she did usually have more opinions than a good girlfriend should."

She wasn't a liar. Wasn't going to start now. She knew exactly what he was referring to. She'd felt that old familiar tug herself, and the years had dropped away.

She looked at him, and even across the table, she felt the heat coming off him, coming off her.

"Yeah, I remember," she said.

The silence was thicker than the chocolate shakes she knew they'd both order and she had no idea what to say to him. How to break the strange atmosphere? Fortunately, the waitress came and they ordered. It didn't take long because neither of them were the, "hold the tomato, I want my pickle on the side, can I substitute salad for fries?" types. They ordered what was on the menu. Simple. Straightforward. Like their relationship used to be.

He drank water, sucked one of the ice cubes into his mouth and chewed it. The gesture mesmerized her. How could he be so gorgeous and so familiar and not hers? She imagined his lips on hers right now, they'd be cold to the touch, his tongue would be icy.

She swallowed and turned her attention to her cutlery, rearranging it just so.

"So, you going to Amanda and Pete's wedding?"

Naturally she'd known he'd be invited since Amanda had been a close friend of both of them in high school. She'd met Pete when she was teaching English in Korea and now they were getting married.

"Yes. I am."

"You taking anyone to the wedding?" he asked around another ice cube. She wanted to lean over and lick the cube rolling around his mouth. She couldn't believe the way her body was playing tricks on her mind like this.

And why was he asking her a question like this? Was he suddenly interested in her again? Going to ask her to be his date for the wedding? A little spurt of something— maybe hope, maybe dread, maybe panic, maybe a little of all three—went through her. "I don't think so."

He nodded, not seeming all that surprised. "Maybe you can save me a dance."

That was it? A dance?

"Sure." Obviously he wasn't looking for a date. Perhaps he was simply making casual conversation. She could play it just as casual.

When their food came, he chowed down with obvious hunger, having practiced for several hours, while she found her appetite less hearty than usual. It was so funny to be with him, doing things they'd done as teens and yet to be across the table from a man who had become a stranger to her in the years since they'd broken up.

"Do you like being a cop as much as you thought you would?" she asked him, partly to make conversation but also because she was genuinely curious. They'd both been so sure of what they wanted—had their childish dreams worked out?

"Absolutely," he answered. "I love it. The work's obviously stressful at times, but I feel like I do some good. Keep the city a little safer." He sipped his chocolate milk shake, reminding her that she'd yet to touch hers. The taste was so familiar, so sweet, that she licked her lips and sucked up more. She glanced up and found his eyes on her mouth with an expression that she recognized.

Lust. Pure lust.

One thing she knew. Maybe they'd parted badly, maybe they hadn't spent any time together in more than ten years, but the heat between them was still there.

He dropped his gaze to his plate. Dragged a French fry

through ketchup. "How about you? Being a lawyer suit you?"

"Absolutely," she said, echoing his earlier answer. "You know how I love a good argument. And I find the work interesting. I'm involved in a lot of different cases so I never get bored."

"That's good," he said. "Boredom will kill you."

She felt as if there was a hidden meaning there. Was he trying to tell her he was bored? Maybe one part of his life was boring, like his love life? Or perhaps he thought her work sounded boring.

Who knew?

She used to be so close to him she could almost read his mind. Now he was a stranger to her. A gorgeous, half-familiar stranger.

"So, what do you think about my brother as a coach?" she asked to get them back to a neutral subject.

"He's a good guy. He works us hard, doesn't put up with any bull. Used to be nobody had time to practice, we'd show up at games and hope to hell nobody got hurt since we don't heal as fast as we all used to. Now, he's getting us working more as a team which is obviously critical if we want to do well at the tournament. He got us thinking about building a team being like building a fort. Frankly, I think we all thought that head injury had done him in. But a few drills that stressed team-building and it started to come together."

"Maybe I'll come and cheer you guys on in Portland," she said. Portland was where the big tournament would be held.

His gaze caught hers and she felt the strength of him, the stunning connection she still felt to him. "That would be great."

They chatted about the team's chances and then the last

of her milk shake was sucked dry, and Greg had eaten both his burger and half of hers. There was nothing to keep them here any longer. But how she hated to let him go.

In the parking lot, there was a moment of hideous awkwardness. Did she hug him? Shake his hand? Kiss him on the cheek?

He seemed equally stuck in uncertainty. Finally, when the moment stretched a little too long, she gave a nervous giggle and opened her arms to hug him.

He took her in, squeezed her to his big body. Then pulled away quickly. "See you around," he said.

She felt as though she could barely breathe. "Yeah," she managed. "See you around."

She drove home. *See you around?* What kind of crap thing was that to say to a person. *See you around.*

She did a few Saturday errands, picked up some things at the organic grocer in her neighborhood. And then went for a run along the path that edged the beach. The air was cool and bracing. The water was gray, the seabirds gray, the distant mountains a darker gray. When rain began to fall she didn't stop. She'd grown up in Vancouver so she was used to it. Besides, the drops were cooling. The exercise helped calm her a bit, but the truth was that since she'd seen Greg this morning she'd felt on edge.

Truth was, she was sexually starved. She hadn't had a man in her life for a while and seeing a specimen of pretty much solid testosterone was reminding all her girlie bits that they'd been starved for too long. That's all it was.

Running helped calm her but it couldn't quench the restless heat coursing through her body.

She jogged back to her apartment, took a long shower.

While she was combing out her hair, her door buzzer went.

She wasn't expecting anyone. She put on her robe and answered the intercom.

"Sam, it's me."

There was only one "me" who could fire her up at the mere sound of his voice uttering a few words over an intercom.

A sweet, familiar ache began low in her belly. "Come on up," she said.

3

GREG HAD NO IDEA WHAT he was doing entering this woman's apartment. He'd argued with himself back and forth since they'd parted in the restaurant parking lot.

But she was like an addictive drug. One taste of her was never going to be enough.

So he'd gone to her place. He knew where it was, like he knew a lot of things about her in the peripheral part of his brain. He wondered if she'd kept the same casual tabs on him over the years.

She wasn't home. He'd been so keyed up to see her, talk to her, something, that the disappointment felt like a blow.

He'd been about to drive away when he saw her jogging toward him, her form still trim, though she'd become a little curvier with time.

He gave her fifteen minutes to shower, thought that ought to be long enough for anyone. Then he called up.

When she answered, he didn't know what to say. Had no idea why he was there. But she didn't seem to care. She'd invited him up, and here he was, outside her door.

He took a deep breath. Raised a hand to knock and to his horror realized it wasn't quite steady. He'd faced down deranged, drugged-up killers, been called to scenes of terrible tragedy, and had always kept a steady head and hand.

Now he was going shaky over a woman? A woman who'd dumped him and pissed all over his broken heart?

He must be losing it.

But that didn't stop him from rapping urgently on her door.

She opened it. She stood before him in a silk robe that barely covered her thighs. The V-neck gave him a tantalizing glimpse of cleavage. Her hair was a damp mess falling down her back.

He stepped inside.

She shut the door.

For a moment they simply stared at each other, then she leaned forward, rose to her toes and put her lips on his. And just like that, lust sucker punched him.

He had his arms around her before he could even think about stopping himself, about restraint, brains, consequences, going down this self-destructive road again with this woman who was as much a part of him and his past as his right arm. With her body rubbing up against him, damp and smelling of all those female potions, and the underlying womanly scent of her, how could he think?

Why would he want to?

Their mouths were greedy for each other, crazy. They kissed the way starving people might eat. His hands were in her hair, fisting in the still damp strands.

She had her hands under the leather jacket he hadn't taken off, pushing it off his shoulders. He stopped to shrug the thing off, to help her yank his shirt over his head.

She touched his naked chest, dipping her head to lick at him. He plunged under that robe, feeling for her, for her breasts that were round and plump and perfect. Oh, so familiar, and yet somehow new. She moaned when he cupped her, nipped at him, and kept going south.

His blood was pounding, need driving him to take, to give. To possess.

Her hands were working at his belt, but his raging erection and his impatience made it torture.

He pushed her hands away, not wanting to waste the time.

He kicked off his shoes, dragged off his socks, and, while she watched him with those amazing big blue-green eyes of hers, yanked his jeans and shorts off in one less-than-smooth move.

Her gaze traveled up and down, drinking him in and he felt a tiny sizzle of embarrassment along with a need stronger than any he'd ever known.

Sam knew she'd never wanted a man more. Not any man. This man. She loved the darkness of his skin, the tight, hard abs, and the glorious cock standing stiff and proud.

His eyes were dark, liquid, heavy with wanting that matched her own. His breathing was ragged. He reached for her and she loved the play of muscles in his arms. There was a scar she'd never seen before on his right bicep. Later, she knew, she'd ask about it. But not now. For now she kissed the jagged spot.

He reached for the belt of her robe, holding her gaze with his, and when he unwrapped her, she felt not as though she and her body had aged a decade since he'd last set eyes on her, but as though she were brand-new.

His gaze traveled down her naked body and he made a sound that could only be satisfaction. She felt beautiful, irresistible and so hot she was about to explode.

Maybe she wanted him enough to take him right now

on the polished concrete floor, but for their first time reunited, she really craved the comfort of her big, expensive bed with the soft linen sheets. She took his hand, led him to her bedroom.

With no ceremony at all, he yanked the pretty duvet back and pushed her to the bed. He joined her there, hot and hard everywhere.

He kissed her again, deeper, licking into her mouth, toying with her. Then he kissed his way to her breasts where he spent a good amount of time and she was hot and restless by the time he moved down her belly, not as athletic as his, but he didn't seem to mind.

Before she quite realized his intention, he was pushing her thighs apart with his tough cop's hands and burying his face in her heat.

Surprise, shock, intense pleasure hit her in a big, swamping wave as he proceeded to use his tongue and lips to savor and delight her.

This wasn't like a first time, she realized, when they'd both been so tentative and unsure of what they were doing. Now they knew each other intimately. She hadn't changed that much in a decade and he knew it. He'd learned on her body as she'd learned on his, and there wasn't an inch of her he hadn't explored, toyed with, figuring out what she liked, how the whole sex thing worked.

It had been so much fun. How could she ever have known there'd never be anyone else who could give her this kind of pleasure?

Maybe because she'd loved him as she'd never loved again.

Her head dropped back against the pillows and she gave herself over to the sensations rioting through her body. Shivering heat, little electric thrills, and a gradually building tension. When he pushed a finger inside her and rubbed unerringly at her G spot, she couldn't hold back the cry that shook her, as her body thrust and rocked against him, spilling over.

"I want you inside me," she said, feeling desperate to be filled.

"Condoms," he gasped.

"I'm on the p—" Of course. With all the years and who knew how many lovers between them, it wasn't only pregnancy he wanted to avoid. How sad.

She leaned over to her bedside drawer, plopped a few on the table and helping herself to one, ripped it open. Sheathing him gave her a chance to touch him, to refamiliarize herself with that part of him that had always fascinated her. So different from anything on her own body, and it had given her so much pleasure.

Once more he parted her thighs. Once more she opened for him. This time he looked into her eyes. The intimacy was so shocking she wanted to look away, but she didn't. Couldn't.

He entered her and she felt the slow slide of pleasure as her body took him in. Little pulses from her first orgasm sent tiny shocks through her.

Wanting to be closer, wanting more, she wrapped her legs around him and pulled him inside her even as he thrust deeper.

It was a fierce mating, two strong, agile bodies thrusting against a shared past, pushing into the present. He had better control now, she noted hazily, as he toyed with her and pleasured her, bringing her up and up, waiting for her.

Their gazes were locked as she came in a glorious rush, and she felt his body climax in tune with hers. The moment was so sweet she wanted it to last forever.

But nothing lasts forever. Not even memory.

He rolled them so that she was snuggled against him. She could hear the bang of his heart begin to slow, his harsh breathing even, and the heat of his skin fade to warm.

Emotion pricked at her eyelids as the rush of remembered love coursed through her body.

"I—" She was panting, lost in a rush of feelings she couldn't even describe. She what?

"Shh," he said, kissing her damp forehead.

And with his arms wrapped protectively around her, she drifted off to sleep.

4

GREG WOKE UP WITH A smile on his face and for that moment right before fully waking, let himself bask in the feelings of a warm, sleeping woman curled in his arms, of the scent of her skin in his nostrils and a dark tendril of her hair lapping his shoulder.

By moving his head an inch he could kiss the nape of her neck, one of his favorite spots on her body, and, as he knew all too well, one of hers.

He'd known he wanted her.

And that was all he'd known.

How could he have expected this complicated rush of emotion? Want edged way too close to need where she was concerned, and passion bumped its head against the residual anger he still experienced when he recalled how they'd parted. The harsh words yelled, the insults, the final door slammed.

What was his crime? He'd asked the woman he loved to marry him.

She was leaving for law school and he understood that the best school was on the other side of the country even as she knew there were good schools a lot closer. But he'd supported her dream, hadn't he? Had he asked her to stay behind?

No, he had not. He'd sucked up his disappointment. Considered briefly traveling out with her, but he couldn't train to be a Vancouver cop anywhere but in Vancouver. It wasn't like he had a choice.

So, she'd made the choice for both of them. And because he loved her, because he didn't want to be separated from her, and he'd wanted her to know that she'd be taking his heart and his hopes and his future with her on that plane, he'd spent all his savings on a ring.

And booked a fancy place for dinner. He thought with a wince that he might have even sprung for red roses, but he was twenty-two. What did he know?

Nothing about that night had gone as planned.

From the second they got to the restaurant he'd started feeling strange. She talked about her new school and how nervous she was about classes and profs and whether she'd be able to keep up, whether she was as smart as she'd always thought she was, whether she had any aptitude for the law.

He'd felt her slipping away.

Maybe that's why he'd fumbled the next part so badly that he still felt squirmy when he thought about it. He'd said something really smooth, like maybe when she came home she'd be too smart for him.

She'd looked at him with surprise. "I thought you were proud of me."

"I am. But I don't want you to get so full of being a lawyer that you forget what's important."

Hurt and a shade of annoyance shaded her eyes. "Are you saying I'm full of myself?" She put her knife and fork down, never a good sign in a woman who loved food.

"No." What was he trying to say? "I love you."

Her expression relaxed. "I love you, too." She reached out and touched his cheek. "It won't be long until Christmas."

"We've never been apart longer than a week. Not since eighth grade."

"I know. I'm really going to miss you." She bit her lip. "I can't afford to come home for Thanksgiving as well as Christmas. But maybe you could fly out for a few days?"

"I start my training course in September. Not sure I'll be able to go."

The ring was burning a hole in his pocket and all he could think about was the joy on her face when she saw it.

"We only have a few days left before I leave." Her voice dropped to husky in a way he loved. "We'd better not waste them."

He thought he would love this woman for the rest of his life. She was his first, his only, and he knew deep in his bones that he'd never want another woman, not with Sam in his life. His buddies had joked around that once Sam was on the other side of the country, he'd be a free man. But he didn't feel that way. Didn't want to be free.

For damn sure didn't want her thinking she was free.

"I know what I want to do," he said, leaning forward, taking her hand.

She leaned in a little, smiled at him with those big ocean-colored eyes. "Is it very kinky?" she purred.

He gulped. *Now or never.* His hand was a little unsteady as he pulled out the ring box. Put it on the table in front of her. "I want to tell all our friends that we'll be getting married as soon as you finish school." He paused for a second. Wondered why they need to wait so long. "Sooner if you want."

She'd stared at that ring box as though it were a live grenade, or a poisonous spider, or an engagement ring from a guy you had no intention of marrying.

Where was the welling of tears in her eyes? The amazed squeal? The excitement?

"Are you asking me to marry you?" she whispered.

"Yeah. I am. I can't wait to tell everybody. They'll be so stoked."

She looked up and as their gazes connected he didn't see love there, but doubt. "But I'm moving to Toronto for three years."

"I know."

"Why wouldn't you wait until I was done school?"

"Because I want to know that every guy on campus will see that ring and know you're taken," he'd blurted. Which wasn't at all what he'd meant to say, but she'd rattled him. Where were the tears? The throwing herself in his arms and promising eternal love? Where was the chick-flick moment he'd imagined?

She hadn't even lifted the box to take a peek. She'd stared at him, her eyes now big and sad. "You don't trust me."

"It's not you I don't trust. It's guys."

Which he now realized wasn't the smartest thing he could have said.

"So, are you going to wear an engagement ring too?" she'd demanded in that pissy voice she got when they talked about feminism and stuff. Like there was only one right answer and he was never going to come up with it. "I know how women like a hot cop."

He'd known her long enough to realize when her mood was dangerous. But he'd been too angry, too humiliated, too hurt that she had so misunderstood him, and he'd picked up the ring box and stuffed it back in his pocket.

"Forget it. Just forget it."

He'd called for the check and they'd left the restaurant, him with a sour taste in his mouth. The eatery was still there, still one of the top restaurants in town. He'd never been back.

The fight they'd had after they left had been their worst ever. When they were done throwing insults at each other—and they both knew each other's weaknesses too well—not only were they not getting married, they weren't even talking.

He held out, stubborn and angry, for five days.

The day that Sam was getting on a plane to Toronto was marked with a big black ring on the family calendar. His mother asked about having Sam and her family over for a goodbye dinner and he came up with some excuse.

Each day he waited for the phone to ring. For Sam to show up and tell him she'd overreacted. She was sorry.

And each day ended with him going to bed in howling frustration.

At last it arrived. The day with the big black ring around it.

She was leaving.

In a panic, he realized that she wasn't going to come crawling back. If he wanted her, he had to go and do the groveling, even though he hadn't done anything wrong.

Truth was he didn't even care, he couldn't let her go without saying goodbye, without trying to make things right. In a panic he'd rushed to her house, but he was too late. They'd already left for the airport.

He'd wanted to write, and didn't have a clue what to say. Waited for her to get hold of him, and his in-box remained Sam-less.

Now here he was, back in her bed, and as the old familiar feelings rushed through him his smile faded. He wondered how he could have been so stupid.

He felt like a drug addict who manages to stay clean and sober for a decade and then one day thinks he's strong enough for one drink. One toke. One hit.

And finds himself as deeply addicted as ever. No twenty-eight-day program would ever help him now.

A decade of sobriety and he was starting down a slippery downward path. If he didn't act fast, he'd be lost forever.

The sleeping woman beside him stirred. She was even more gorgeous than she'd been at twenty-two if that was possible. Her mouth was a little firmer and there was a tiny fan of crows' feet around her eyes that were new to him, but she had grown into herself. Instead of bravado, she now had true confidence. Her body had filled out nicely and in all the right places. She looked, smelled, tasted fantastic…familiar.

Greg raised a hand to smooth her hair back off her face and let it drop, not wanting to wake her. She was so peaceful sleeping. Not arguing or stating her case or in some way trying to piss him off. He realized how much he'd missed her.

Not just the sex, which had never been as good.

He'd wondered over the years if his memory might be faulty because no woman, and there'd been a few, had ever felt as right in his bed as Sam. Maybe he'd never experienced the highs he and Sam had reached together because they were each other's first, and he'd built that time up in his memory to some lofty height that reality could never achieve.

Making love with her again had been—if possible— better than he remembered. They both had a little more maturity and experience but it was something beyond that.

Something elemental with them, as though they knew each other's bodies and needs as well as they knew their own. Instinctively. It was weird. But in a good way.

He lay on his side, watching her sleep. It wasn't just the sex, there was some magical quality between them that had always been there. That he'd never believed he'd find again.

What was it? And why with this woman and only this one?

A pain pierced his chest so quickly he thought for a second he was having a heart attack.

And in a way he supposed he was. Because the truth, when it hit him, was inescapable.

He was still in love with this woman. Had loved her since before he understood what love was, had believed in them enough to propose marriage when she headed off for university.

He'd so carefully avoided her for years and his plan had been working. He got on with his life, she got on with hers and if they happened to bump into each other—between high-school weddings and the fact that her brother was his best friend—they dealt.

When it did happen that they found themselves in the same house or garden or wedding chapel, he'd made sure they had the minimum possible contact.

So why, today, had he thrown away a decade of self-protection?

Since when had he become self-destructive?

And now that he was on this dangerous path, now that he'd fallen so spectacularly off the wagon, what the hell was he going to do about it?

He knew there was only one thing he could do.

With a weight of sadness that felt like an anvil on his chest, he pressed a whisper-soft kiss on her shoulder blade and then rolled soundlessly out of bed.

5

SAM WOKE WITH A SLOW, satisfied smile. Not even wanting to open her eyes so she could savor the memories of the night before.

She stretched her arms over her head, pointed her toes and stretched her lower half, enjoying the feeling of being in her body. Of everything that body could do, had done, had experienced and enjoyed through that long, delicious night.

She turned and reached for Greg. Wanting to tell him— she didn't even know what—but wanting him to know how special it had been, the day that had stretched into night. They'd been so starved for each other.

A sweet tingle went through her as she thought about him.

Amazingly, she still wasn't satisfied.

Her questing arms hit cold sheets. Puzzled, she opened her eyes. She glanced around and squinted at the clock. It was almost nine. She hadn't slept this long on a Sunday morning in ages. But then she hadn't been this relaxed in ages.

She remembered trying to speak, to tell Greg how much she'd missed him, but he'd looked at her with that smile in his eyes that told her everything she needed to know, and then he'd sent her to sleep with a kiss.

He was so sweet. And she was so happy to have him back.

The bathroom door was shut so she raised her voice. "Hey, lover boy. I think I'm out of food. How 'bout I take us out for breakfast?"

He didn't answer. She raised her voice louder. "I hope you made coffee."

With a huge yawn, she rolled herself out of bed, shuffled into her robe and pushed her feet into fuzzy gray slippers.

When she padded out to the kitchen she experienced her first twinge of doubt. The coffeepot was cold. The kitchen, pristine.

And as her senses sharpened she realized that she didn't hear anything or even have that notion of another person being in her place.

And then she saw the note.

A bright yellow Post-it slapped in the middle of her fridge like a pimple on a forehead. It read:

Thanks for last night.
You're the best.
G

She read the note. Once. Then she read it again. And again, but the obscurity of the message didn't change. Nor could she squeeze any more meaning out of it.

Thanks for last night? Like she'd done him a favor? Changed the oil on his car or picked up his dry cleaning?

You're the best. While she naturally agreed with the literal translation of the words, it was the sort of phrase you'd throw out to a waitress who brought you an extra side of toast, or someone who'd done you a favor, such as changing your oil or picking up your dry cleaning.

Somebody with whom you'd had the best sex ever? In your whole pathetic life? *Thanks for last night. You're the best,* wasn't cutting it.

Even the signature was abbreviated. Deliberately casual. G. Like writing three more letters would have killed him?

And where was the part about calling her, or seeing her again?

Because she was a lawyer and tried to consider all sides, she actually peeled the note off the fridge and flipped it over. As though there might be more on the other side. But it was as cheerfully, blankly yellow as one of those little smiley faces.

By the time the coffee had brewed and she was sipping her first mug of the day, she realized that he'd very deliberately avoided any mention of calling her. Or seeing her again.

That note was telling her she'd had a one-night stand. No promises. No expectations.

No implied future.

She ripped the note a few times. Then she tossed the little pieces. They floated to the trash like jagged yellow confetti for a wedding that would never happen.

For the strangest moment, she felt like crying. Standing there in her designer kitchen, drinking her fair trade coffee in a sleek black mug, she felt like crying.

But Sam wasn't one to give in that easily.

If Greg wanted to pretend that what had happened between them was nothing a Post-it note couldn't fix, then that was fine.

She wasn't a girl who stood in her kitchen crying in

her coffee because a man had left before she was ready for him to leave. Before they'd even had a conversation she'd assumed would happen over breakfast.

It was as though they'd reached a place of complete physical intimacy while emotionally they'd avoided contact as much as possible.

And now he was gone.

Fine.

She was fine.

She was a modern, independent, successful single woman. She'd enjoyed some great sex. What wasn't great about that? So, the guy didn't happen to want a future. Or commitment. Fine!

Instead of standing around whining, she did what she always did when emotion threatened to swamp her.

She pulled on her running gear and headed out.

The day was unexpectedly sunny. As she pounded down her regular route, toward the beach, she saw families headed for church, computer hounds and university students hunched over their screens in Starbucks, forgotten mugs at their sides. She waved to Mike, the homeless guy who pushed the crosswalk button when he saw her coming so she wouldn't have to wait.

This was her world. Her life.

She'd made it what she wanted and nobody was going to mess with that. Nobody.

Her work was absorbing, she liked her firm and her colleagues, her apartment was sleek and modern and low-maintenance, so she could lock up and head out on a moment's notice if she felt like heading to Whistler for a weekend's skiing, or hitting any exotic destination.

The breath was rasping in her lungs and she realized that she was running too fast. She slowed down, tried to find her pace.

She had friends, family, good local restaurants, and if she felt lonely there were people she called.

Sure, Greg had stirred up some old longings, reminded her of the future she'd once thought she'd have.

No wonder she felt off, slightly melancholy. It was impossible to go back. She should have known that. She had to keep her eyes firmly forward. On the future.

With that in mind, after her run, she stretched, showered and then threw her sheets into the wash and changed the bed. She had a cleaning service, but it still felt good to rid the apartment of all traces of where Greg had been.

Then, dressed in jeans, a crisp white shirt and a navy blazer, she went in to work.

There was something soothing about the office on a Sunday afternoon. A couple of other lawyers were around, but mostly the space was silent, without the shrill of phones, the noise and commotion of busy lawyers and support staff.

She could always absorb herself in her work. By writing up a brief and catching up on some correspondence, she passed a few hours.

She had the fleeting idea that maybe she'd call Jarrad and see what his plans were for dinner, but pride stopped her. He and Greg were best friends. What if Greg had talked to him? Besides, he had Sierra, and anyway, she'd always been the kind of person who worked things out for herself.

In the end she called a divorced colleague who she knew hated Sunday nights on his own and they went out for sushi and a movie. By listening to his problems, she was able to put her own aside for an evening.

When she crawled into bed that night after the news, she could have sworn she still smelled Greg in her bedding. Which was ridiculous since she'd thrown all traces

Get 2 Books FREE!

Harlequin® Books,
publisher of women's fiction,
presents

GET 2 BOOKS

We'd like to send you two *Harlequin® Blaze®* novels absolutely free. Accepting them puts you under no obligation to purchase any more books.

HOW TO GET YOUR 2 FREE BOOKS AND 2 FREE GIFTS

1. Return the reply card today, and we'll send you two *Harlequin Blaze* novels, absolutely free! We'll even pay the postage!

2. Accepting free books places you under no obligation to buy anything, ever. Whatever you decide, the free books and gifts are yours to keep, free!

3. We hope that after receiving your free books you'll want to remain a subscriber, but the choice is yours—to continue or cancel, any time at all!

EXTRA BONUS

You'll also get two free mystery gifts! (worth about $10)

FREE!

of him into the laundry. Still, she passed a restless night and even though she didn't remember her dreams she had a bad feeling that she knew who had haunted them.

For the next few days she didn't sleep all that well, which really pissed her off. Otherwise, life went on as normal. Greg didn't contact her.

Fine.

Wednesday she put in a long day, having spent a few frustrating hours in court where the judge didn't see things quite her way. Always annoying.

So she wasn't at her best when she stepped off the elevator and walked to her door that Wednesday evening.

She was putting her key in the lock when a man's voice said, from right behind her, "Hello, Sam."

She didn't stop to think but acted on pure instinct. She pulled out the key and flipped up the Mace can she kept on her key ring to spray in her attacker's face.

She was about to let him have it when it registered that this was Greg standing there, and he simultaneously yelled, "Sam, it's me."

Adrenaline was still pumping as she lowered her hand slowly. "What are you doing here?"

She was feeling pissy enough with him that she almost wished she'd let him have a good blast of Mace before she'd recognized him.

"I came to see you," he said warily, still watching her hands. "You going to put that away?"

"Haven't decided yet."

She narrowed her eyes. "How did you get in here? It's a secure building."

He pulled out his shield. "Told your doorman it was police business."

"You planning to arrest me?"

He huffed out a sigh that sounded like pure frustration.

Now she looked at him and she got the feeling he wasn't sleeping very well either. There was a pinched expression around his eyes and circles beneath them. "Maybe. Do you think we could go inside and talk?"

Once again she inserted her key in her lock. Opened the door. She entered and he followed.

She didn't invite him in, merely put down her bag on the floor and confronted him. "What do you want?"

"This," he said, and, pulling her against him, took possession of her mouth.

No, she wanted to yell. *No, this isn't what I want,* but she was already lost. The second his lips touched hers she felt the tide of longing sweep over her, beginning in her core and radiating out to her very pores.

"You make me mental," he murmured in her ear as he yanked off her coat, letting it drop unheeded to the floor and pushing her against the wall.

She had her hands at his zipper, working it down. "I know."

He reached under the hem of her skirt, felt for her panties, slipped a hand inside and she knew she was already wet for him.

"Oh, you feel so good."

Their gazes connected and she saw reflected all the emotions she was feeling. Sadness, longing, frustration and a kind of horniness that was almost too strong. Like a raging fever.

As though he couldn't bear to have his emotions hanging out there for her to read, he suddenly turned her and stripped her panties and stockings down in one forceful move. She had to kick off her heels so he could complete the job, and then he was behind her, the heat from his body warming her all the way to her marrow.

He must have come prepared for she heard the rip of a

condom package and then felt him, hard and ready behind her. She parted her thighs, pushing her hips back against him even as she pressed against the wall for support.

He entered her swift and hard and, oh, it was exactly what her mood wanted.

"Yes," she almost growled, pushing back against him as he began to pump against her. She felt the friction increase, heard his breathing grow ragged, her own panting, then he grabbed her hips, pulling her back against him so their flesh began to slap together.

Oh, it was so good, and he reached places inside her that no one else ever had.

Ever would.

She still wore her blazer from work, her elegant blue silk shirt, and here she was, a woman who billed out at more than three hundred dollars an hour, with her skirt up around her waist being taken roughly from behind by a man who worked the more basic side of the law.

He pulled the pins holding her loose bun in place and her hair cascaded around her shoulders. He kissed it, pushed his lips through it to reach her neck and then, to her shock, she felt him bite her, right at the joint of shoulder and neck, like a stallion mounting a mare.

The swift jolt of pain was soothed by his tongue. His heat surrounded her, the scent of him, of them together. Her senses were swimming, her legs becoming unsteady.

And then he reached around her hips, touched a finger to her hot spot and began to play with her using the same rhythm as his thrusting cock.

She turned her head, greedy for his mouth, and found him there. He took her mouth, she took his, as they swallowed each others' wild cries.

And then they both slid to the floor. Her skirt was a

wrinkled mess, his pants still around his ankles, but they didn't care. They held each other, catching their breath.

He ran his hands idly through her hair and a memory surged to the surface. A time when they'd been studying together and had stopped to make love, and afterward she remembered him stroking her hair in exactly this way while they discussed the play they were studying. They'd even read each other some of the choice lines.

"You said you'd die for me," she said softly, remembering.

"What?" He lifted his head and looked down at her, utterly confused.

"Remember? When we were studying *Romeo and Juliet*. We were the only two who really understood the play and why those two killed themselves rather than live without the other. You said you'd die for me."

Sadness filled his eyes and she felt him withdrawing. "That was a long time ago."

Silence filled her apartment. He eased away and, rising, pulled his pants up and zipped and belted. She straightened her skirt and got to her feet, not wanting to be at a disadvantage looking up at him from the floor.

She knew he was leaving and pride refused to let her ask him to stay.

"Maybe I did," he said, his hand on the doorknob.

"Maybe you did what?"

He glanced back and his expression was closed. "Die for you."

6

BEFORE SHE COULD ASK Greg for an explanation, he was gone.

She felt like screaming with frustration. Not only from his cryptic comment about dying for her, but from the frustration of a woman who's had an after-work quickie and wants much, much more.

Sometimes, she was really glad she had a big brother, especially now he was in town. She no longer cared that he was Greg's best friend. She needed Jarrad's counsel.

She called him and Jarrad told her to swing by his house. In minutes she'd showered, changed into jeans and a cherry-red sweater, slipped on boots and her leather jacket and headed out. As always, the drive to Jarrad's soothed her. From Kitsilano, she skirted English Bay, driving down Point Grey Road, then taking the Burrard Street Bridge, edging around downtown Vancouver and over the Lions Gate Bridge and then taking the scenic, if slower, Marine Drive. The highway would be quicker but she felt the need to gather her thoughts. She needed a strong male shoulder to lean on, but she also needed to figure out how much to tell a nosy family member.

There was something about the timeless beat of the ocean that made any problem seem smaller.

When she pounded on Jarrad's door she smelled something amazing. He opened the door and she was struck by how happy he looked, how relaxed. "Hey, sis," he said, pulling her in for a bear hug.

"Bro." She hugged him back.

"Sierra's here, but we can go for a walk if you want some privacy."

"I know she's here. Nothing you can cook smells that good," she said, walking into the room and giving her favorite schoolteacher a hug. "What's for dinner?"

Sierra also seemed to have bloomed in the weeks she'd known Jarrad. The woman had an inner confidence that had been lacking. Looking at the pair, she thought they were one of those rare couples who truly fitted together.

Imagine.

"Chicken cacciatore. Enough for three."

She grinned. "I'd love you even if you hadn't straightened out my brother. I'll set the table."

"Wine?" Jarrad brandished a bottle of red.

"Sure."

The three of them sat around the fireplace which danced with the flames of a real wood fire. Jarrad handed out the wine and she sipped gratefully.

She glanced around at the mishmash of handmade furniture and the blue-and-white upholstery. Sure, it was charming, but with this property right on the ocean, he could have a real showplace. "I hope you're going to knock this shack down and build a real house now Sierra's in the picture," she said.

She caught the shared glance between her dinner hosts and knew instinctively that was never going to happen. Had he actually found a woman who preferred sea shanty to luxury? She shook her head. "You really are perfect for him, aren't you?"

"Yep," her brother said, putting an arm around his woman.

"Jarrad said you sounded upset," Sierra said, giving her a concerned look. "If you want to talk, I can go in the other room."

She waved a hand. "No. You're a woman. Maybe you can help."

She took a sip of wine. Jarrad always had great wine. She took another approving sip.

"What's up?"

"I've sort of been seeing Greg."

Jarrad choked on his wine. "You have?"

Sierra, she noted, didn't look at all surprised. She was one of those quiet, smart women who didn't miss much.

"Well, that's the problem, actually. I'm not seeing him, only sleeping with him."

"Slut!" Jarrad said in mock disgust.

She leaned over and punched his knee.

"Ow," he said, laughing. "Okay, okay. You're sleeping with the dude. Get it. You're both single, I don't see the problem."

Sierra shook her head. "Men never do."

"I know." She turned to the woman she strongly suspected would soon be her sister-in-law. "I'm not sure if you know, but we used to go out in high school."

The other woman nodded. "I heard."

"He wanted to marry me when I left to go back east to law school. I thought he was trying to control me and we had this huge fight and broke up. You know, the kind of fight that you figure you'll settle because in your whole life you've always worked it out and moved on?"

Sierra nodded.

"But this one we somehow never did. And the more time that passed, the more impossible it was for us to patch things up."

A log popped in the fireplace and she thought how cozy it was here. They didn't even have music playing so she heard the ocean beating against the shore. She shook her head. "A decade can go by real fast. And then we met again at the rink and went for a burger and, boom, we ended up in bed so fast I was still tasting French fries."

She frowned as the memory played out all the way. "And then he left. Without saying anything about seeing me again."

"Did it happen only the one time?"

"No. It's been a couple of times. It's like he can't stay away from me, but he doesn't want a real relationship with me either."

"What set off the panic phone call?" Jarrad wanted to know.

"I was feeling weird, you know? And I reminded him that when we read *Romeo and Juliet* in high school he'd said he would die for me."

"Sounds like a sixteen-year-old," Jarrad said.

"Be quiet, Jarrad," Sierra said in her schoolteacher voice. "How did Greg respond?"

"He said, maybe he already did die for me. What kind of a stupid thing is that to say to a person? I don't even know what it means."

"Are you sure?" The gentle voice prodded.

Instead of answering, Sam drank some more wine. "Maybe. Maybe it means I killed his love for me."

"Oh, I don't think so. I don't think so at all."

"You mean…?" She didn't even want to finish the sentence, didn't want to admit to anyone in the room, least of all herself, how much she wanted it to be true that Greg still loved her.

"I think he still loves you. You remember how *Romeo and Juliet* ends?"

"In a bloodbath," Jarrad said with a frown. "Or was that *Hamlet?*"

Sierra ignored him. "Juliet's taken this potion to make it seem as though she's dead so she can supposedly be buried in the family vault, and then she'll wake up and sneak out and live happily ever after with Romeo. But he never gets the message so when he hears she has died, he truly believes she's gone. Romeo can't live without her, and so he kills himself at her side."

"Right. I remember the play."

"But then Juliet wakes up and finds Romeo dead. And in despair she kills herself with his sword so they can be together always."

"Right. Tragic teenaged love."

Sierra gazed into the fire and the light pinkened her cheeks. "The play's also about miscommunication. Sometimes speaking the truth is the most important thing you can do."

"But if his love is dead…"

"Not his love. His pride. His ego. Greg threw himself on his sword, metaphorically, when he proposed to you and you turned him down. Right now, I'd say you're at the part of the play where you're waking up and discovering he's made this huge sacrifice for you. Question is, what are you going to do about it?"

"Are you suggesting I should—what was your expression—throw myself on my sword?"

"It's up to you what you do. But the rest of your life is a long time to go without the man you love."

She didn't even protest that she still loved the guy. Not

when Sierra was so smart. What was the point? "So I have to propose?"

"Sacrifice your ego and pride on the altar of love and see what happens."

Sam felt a little sick. "But what if he says no?"

"You won't be any worse off than you are now. And at least you'll know."

At least she'd know.

"I don't know. I have to think about this. Maybe it would be better if I told him not to come around anymore. Go back to the way things were."

No one answered her. After a beat of silence, Jarrad said, "I'm starved. Let's eat." And the emotional part of the evening ended with them all heading to the table, passing bread and sharing Sierra's amazing food.

"Mmm, this is fantastic," Sam said as she dug into the meal Sierra had prepared. She might be broken-hearted, but she could still enjoy a hearty meal. She ripped apart a slice of bread and before she stuck a piece in her mouth, said to her brother, "You'd better not let this woman get away."

"I don't intend to," Jarrad said, giving Sierra a secret, intimate smile that made Sam's heart ache. Not that she wanted to deny them their obvious bliss with each other, but because she wanted some of that herself.

She twirled pasta around her fork then, before she filled her mouth, said, "Have you ever done something that if you could undo it, would change your whole life for the better?"

"I wish I'd never gone out on the ice on that November away game," Jarrad said immediately. She knew how hard that had been for him, suffering a career-ending hit before he was ready to retire.

"Oh, boy," she said, reaching out to pat his hand.

"But," he continued, "if I hadn't lost my career I wouldn't have come home right when I did and I wouldn't have met Sierra." He sent his girlfriend another of those intimate glances that made Sam crazy jealous wanting that for herself. "So, no. I'm glad things happened as they did."

"Oh, sweetheart," Sierra said, leaning over to kiss his cheek.

"What about you, Sierra?"

"I would have wished that I never got involved with Michael, a man who didn't deserve me. But then, if I hadn't, I wouldn't have got my heart broken and the girls wouldn't have talked me into playing hockey, and I wouldn't have met Jarrad."

"Yeah, great. This is all really nice, but my wish is that I hadn't turned Greg down when he asked me to marry him. How has that turned out to be a good thing?"

There was a moment of silent. Jarrad looked at her with pity. "Nope. Sorry. Can't help you. You screwed up royally with that one."

"Oh, don't listen to him," Sierra said, half laughing. "You obviously weren't ready to make that kind of commitment when he first asked you." She reached over and gave Sam's wrist a reassuring squeeze. "Now, I think maybe you are."

"But I have to humiliate myself somehow."

"Seems like it."

She shoved the pasta in her mouth. Talked around it. "That sucks."

7

BY THE TIME SHE LEFT Sierra and Jarrad's place Sam had accepted the inevitable.

She loved Greg. Had always loved him and would never love anyone else.

So where did that leave her?

Seemed to her she had two choices. She could continue as things were, knowing that Greg and she would continue sleeping together because she didn't think either of them could stop.

Or she could risk everything and try to win him back—not just in her bed—but all the way.

Husband, babies, home in the suburbs all the way.

According to Sierra, she had to humiliate herself in order to convince the man she loved that she was serious. She wasn't sure about that. Maybe she could tell him her feelings. Surely that would be enough?

But it hadn't been enough for her. Ten years ago Greg had given her exactly that. A proposal of love and marriage and she hadn't believed him.

Now, ten years later, he was older and more cynical. Why would he believe that she loved him simply because she told him so?

He wouldn't.

Instinctively, she knew, he wouldn't.

What could she do to show him?

A slow smile began to form. She had exactly the perfect scenario in mind.

GREG WAS HAVING A BAD day. His fingers banged the keyboard in his own hunt-and-peck style. Not for the first time, he wished he'd taken typing at school. Somehow he'd never imagined that so much of police work would involve clerical duties. As he sat at his regulation desk in the precinct typing another regulation report into his computer, he fumed. Their evidence hadn't held up in court and so a notorious drug dealer and gangbanger had gone free.

He had far too much paperwork to get through in his entire lifetime and his favorite lunch-time eatery had been out of his favorite sandwich.

It even seemed noisier than usual. More cops seemed to be desk-bound, either typing, on the phone or talking amongst themselves. Somebody was organizing a fantasy league, which seemed to involve a lot of joking around, but he had no interest in betting on hockey. He'd rather play it.

So he wasn't in the best of moods when, around four in the afternoon, a pair of black heels strode into his line of vision.

The stilettos were attached to a nice pair of legs and so his eyes naturally followed the line up to the hem of a blue trench coat snugged around a great figure. One he knew well.

Sam's.

She grinned at him when they made eye contact.

"How did you get in here?" he asked.

She wasn't fooled by his gruff manner, he could tell. Her smile only turned saucier.

"I showed the desk sergeant my business card and explained that I needed to see you on an urgent business matter. He let me come up. Professional courtesy."

"Lawyers." He shook his head, automatically saving his work. "What do you want?"

He knew there was interest from everybody in the department since the noise level had immediately dropped to tomblike. Who was this woman and why was she here?

He was wondering that himself. This was his workplace, not her apartment in the dark where no one had to know what was going on.

He didn't feel like explaining to anyone—least of all himself—what exactly was going on. Mostly because he didn't have a clue.

She leaned closer. "I wanted you to know that under this trench coat I am wearing nothing but a light dusting of talcum powder, and that I will be having a drink at that cop bar down the street where you all hang out. If you care to join me."

"Which bar?" He wanted to hear her say the words with that red-lipsticked mouth.

A tiny smile tilted that glorious red. "In The Sin Bin."

The Sin Bin was the slang name for the penalty box in hockey. Also, he supposed a fitting reference to jail. Maybe that's why the cops liked to hang out there, though he figured it was mostly about the proximity to the cop shop and the cold beer and excellent burgers.

Then she turned, and putting extra oomph in her hips, strutted out without giving him a chance to say a word. Which was just as well since his tongue was glued to the roof of his mouth and he couldn't have spoken if he'd been able to think of a thing to say.

He gave her a ten-minute head start. He cleaned up his desk and made his to-do list for the morning so his coworkers wouldn't guess that he was running after a girl in a trench coat, so desperate for her he could barely draw breath. And then he followed her.

When he walked in he saw a couple of guys he knew. Nodded. His eyes scanned the place rapidly. A hockey game was on the big screen, but he couldn't have said what teams were playing. All his focus was on finding that woman.

He caught a flash of blue and followed it to a booth in a corner.

She had a glass of white wine in front of her. A beer in a frosty mug already waiting on the other side of the table. His side.

He sat. Picked up the mug. Drank deeply.

Put down the glass and looked over at her. She wore extra makeup, he noticed, and she'd done her hair in loose curls. She looked like a spy girl.

"What's your plan?" he asked.

Under the table she ran her high-heel-clad foot up the inside of his leg. He swallowed hard. "It's National Seduce a Cop Day. I'm doing my civic duty," she informed him in a low voice.

She was crazy and gorgeous, and he wanted her so bad he could hardly stand it. But over the years he'd learned a little self-control.

He picked up his drink and came around to her side of the booth. As he sat beside her he eyed the tiny gap at her trench coat's hem. "Open your legs," he said softly.

A tiny moan came from deep in her throat. She eased open her thighs and as she did so the coat gapped, giving

him the view he wanted, all the way to paradise. So, he'd
hooked up with an old flame. He wasn't the first. He still
thought she was hot, they had fantastic chemistry and,
until something better came along for either of them, this
arrangement was perfect. Friends with benefits, wasn't
that what they called it?

He sipped his beer and pretended to watch the big
screen while he slipped his hand onto her knee and let
it trail up her inner thigh. She was already trembling.
"Where will this civic duty take place?" he asked.

"Anywhere you like."

"Your place or mine. Somewhere where nobody will
bother us when I make you come so hard you scream."

8

"IT DIDN'T WORK!"

Samantha was close to tears when she met Sierra for coffee the next morning.

"What didn't work?"

"What you said. I totally put myself out there. I showed up at Greg's work in a trench coat, high heels and nothing else. In front of all his colleagues. We went to the bar and he was half-crazy wanting me. Then I took him home and we had the best sex." She shivered at the memory. She put her head in her hand. "But nothing's changed."

Sierra looked at her the way she'd probably look at a second grader who got simple arithmetic all wrong. "Did you really think it would?"

Sam jerked up in her chair. "Yes. I thought it would. You were the *Romeo and Juliet* expert. You told me all I had to do was put myself out there, be prepared to make a fool of myself in the name of love. I'm telling you it didn't work."

Sierra was soft-spoken, a lady, the kind of woman who always let other people go first in lineups. But Sam was beginning to realize she had a streak of steel in her too. And it showed now.

"You played a fun sex game and seduced a man. How is that putting everything on the line and telling him you love him and want to spend the rest of your life with him?"

Sam felt like pouting. Probably she was. "I thought he'd read between the lines."

"If you really want this man, I think you're going to have to try harder." Sierra took a sip of her latte and settled back in her chair. "I don't think you only hurt his pride when you turned down his proposal. I think you genuinely broke his heart."

"Why does everyone keep acting like this is all my fault? I was twenty-two. Headed for law school. I wasn't ready to get married."

"Did you tell him that?"

She squirmed a bit in her chair. Made a production of sweeping some stray specks of sugar off the tabletop. Finally she admitted, "No."

"What did you do?"

"I was under a lot of stress. I was about to leave home and leave everyone I knew, including Greg. And then he threw a ring at me. I did what any woman in my position would do. I freaked."

"Well."

"But he knew me. Better than anyone. All he had to do was write or call. I'd have calmed down, things would have gone back to normal. It was totally his fault."

"Did you ever think about contacting him?"

"Sure, I thought about it."

"And did you?"

"No. I wasn't the one who screwed everything up."

"Are you sure?" The calm voice wasn't accusing, simply asking.

Sam scowled into her coffee and refused to answer.

"Sam, you can't have a relationship where you are

always right. It's statistically impossible. Sometimes, you are wrong. Even worse, sometimes you have to admit you were wrong."

A group of moms with toddlers in tow came in, obviously after some sort of mom-and-tot activity. One kid dragged a green sippy cup, one whined about wanting a cookie. Sam had never felt a single tick from her supposed biological clock. Had assumed she didn't have one. But suddenly she knew she did want kids. And she wanted them with Greg. A man who would take her offer of seducing a cop, but didn't seem interested in much else. "But—I don't know how much more I've got in me."

"Depends how much you want him, I guess."

"Oh, I want him."

"Forever?"

She didn't even hesitate. "Forever."

"Then you'd better think of something."

GREG WAS SO BUSY preparing for the police and firefighter hockey tourney that she barely saw him. He dropped by a couple of times after work or practice, but it was only for a few hours of sex and then he was gone.

She'd start to feel used except that she was enjoying sex as she hadn't enjoyed it in years. Every time they came together she became more convinced that they needed to put their differences aside and commit.

She wanted lots of things that she saw happening with Greg. She pictured a home, a real home like the kind she'd grown up in, him doing lawn-mowing and hand man projects, her slowing down her practice to spend time with her children.

Damn it, she wanted to marry the man.

And now that she was ready, he didn't seem to want to marry her.

He was leaving for the big tourney on Tuesday. It was Saturday night. He hadn't mentioned her coming down to support the team, and she hadn't brought it up. So far their affair was a dark secret. She hadn't told anyone except Jarrad and Sierra and if Greg hadn't told his best friend, then he probably hadn't told anyone.

He arrived at ten as they'd arranged and no sooner had she opened the door to him than he had her in his arms, pushing her inside and kissing her deeply. She could feel his passion and need and, as usual, they fueled her own. By the time he'd pressed her against the hallway wall, his arousal was fierce.

"Oh, baby, I want you so much."

She'd planned to sit him down and talk to him, but she was a woman with strong needs and this man always reminded her of how strong her needs were.

"Bedroom," she panted, "I put on fresh sheets."

He didn't answer, simply bent down and hoisted her into his arms. She squealed and then laughed as he hauled her off to the bedroom holding her tight to his chest. In anticipation of his visit, she was wearing a sexy black nightgown. He put her on the bed and, eyes never leaving her, ripped off his clothes in record speed. She loved his haste, his obvious need for her. Desire filled the air between them.

Greg gazed down at the woman waiting for him on the bed. There was no light in the room save a dim glow from the window, so she was more shadow than real, like a black-and-white photograph. She wore some kind of black lacy thing and under it he could see black panties. A rage of lust pulled at him and he stripped rapidly until he was naked. On the bed. He pulled her against him.

He hadn't realized how intense his need would be, would continue to be no matter how many times he tried to slake it with the woman he was in love with—the woman he'd loved for years.

She kissed him, and it was like his first kiss ever. He leaned into it, into her, and she responded with her usual eagerness. He reached for her, tracing her firm breasts beneath the black silk.

She ran her hands over his bare chest, his belly, then began to touch him as he reached to rub her through her silk panties.

Her breath hissed as he caressed her, feeling the heat pulsing from her. Too eager for finesse, he plunged his hand into her panties, needing to feel her, soft and slick and ready.

"I need…" he gasped. "I need you."

"Yes. Oh, yes."

He began kissing her and rolled her, wanting to be on top of her, but she had the same idea, bossy woman that she was and she kept going.

They tumbled off the bed and onto the floor—her expensively carpeted floor.

"I really, really need to see you," he said.

She kissed him again, rolling on top of him and straddling him. He felt her shift, lean up and flip on a light.

He blinked, and blinked again as the black-and-white photo became woman.

"You are so beautiful," he said, gazing up at her, her hair spilling around her face.

"Stay there. I forgot the condoms." He knew she kept them in the bathroom. He watched her, reminding himself of all the parts of her body he liked so much. The sweet round ass, the thighs that were muscular and sexy from all the running she did, as he was reminded every time they gripped him.

The long line of her back, and the strong shoulders.

Hair, eyes, lips, breasts, belly, hips, all of her added up to such an amazing package. No wonder he couldn't seem to stay away.

She returned with a couple of condoms, ripped one open with her teeth and sheathed him with her own hands. She took her time about it, sneaking in a caress or two, as though she was enjoying learning his body again as much as he was enjoying relearning hers. He tried to stay cool, but it was tough feeling her magic touch, oh, she knew him so well. Knew exactly what he liked. He stayed where he was, on his back, trying to hold himself in check, feeling the soft wool of the carpet rubbing his spine.

She straddled him slowly, and he watched intently as she gripped him in her hand and guided him to the entrance to her body. He barely breathed as she lowered herself slowly onto him, inching him slowly into paradise.

When she'd settled all the way, and he was as deep inside her as he could go, he gripped her hips, holding her against him so he could savor that first moment of complete connection.

He felt her heat, her snug, wet heat and the connection running between them that was so much more than physical. Their gazes caught and held, and he saw vulnerability flash. Something pulled, deep inside him as he realized that he hadn't ever connected so deeply with anyone. Ever.

And then she closed her eyes against him. He felt a slight shudder run through her body, and she was moving, riding him. He caught her rhythm and stayed with her, touching her as she rode him, touching her everywhere, her breasts, her hips, and, when he saw her eyes start to lose their focus, he touched her clit, rubbing it the way he knew she liked. When her head fell back on a cry, he thrust up, up and up inside her, pushing her over the edge, and then following in a spurt of intense pleasure that seemed to get stronger every time.

"Wow," Sam panted as she slumped in a heap on top of Greg, her silk nightie bunched between them. She felt his heart thud beneath her breast. "Wow, wow, wow."

She was usually good with words, but right now, *Wow* seemed to express everything she felt.

Greg drew idle patterns on her back with his fingertips and she let herself enjoy the sensation and the utter relaxation in her body at this moment.

"You know what I want?" he mumbled against her hair.

"You want more?" She raised her head to glare down at him.

He grinned slowly, showing more of his teeth by the second. "I want to try that again with you naked."

The relaxation that had enveloped her a moment past was gone as a familiar tension in her lower body built again.

"And this time," he said, rising to his feet and taking her hand to pull her up with him, "I think we should give the big soft bed a try."

"You getting old?" she teased.

"Definitely." And he pushed her back until she was lying on the bed gazing up at him.

Then he kissed her as though they were sharing their first-ever kiss. He touched her lips gently with his own, moving his mouth over hers, warming her lips before touching her tongue lightly with his. His restraint and sweetness charmed her and she followed his lead, licking at him slowly, kissing as though they weren't going any further than a kiss.

Oh, she'd forgotten how kissing could turn her on. Soon, the restless energy was pulsing through her again.

She wanted more. More of his mouth, more of his body, more of the friction that would send her flying.

Her breathing grew heavy, her body restless, and still he kissed only her mouth in that soft, teasing way. After a long, long time, he kissed his way to her breasts, kissing the slopes, the undersides and finally the sensitive tips. His tongue flicked over her nipple and she felt the charge right to her toes. While his mouth was busy at her breasts, his hands stroked her sides, her belly, her thighs and then settled between her legs.

He followed the path of his hands with his mouth until he was settled between her parted legs and his mouth hovered over her. His moist breath stirred her curls.

Then she didn't think anything at all because he put his mouth on her and put the same slow, restrained patience into licking her as he'd put into kissing her.

With the first rush of passion spent, she could enjoy a slower build, feel the pressure and moisture of his tongue, the way he explored even as he excited. She built slowly, and then faster, until her hips were gyrating and her hands fisting against the bedclothes.

So close.

He moved up her body and she would have begged him to take her if she didn't feel him already there, not so lazy now, not so slow. But he still took the time to look deeply into her eyes as he entered her slowly and completely.

Lust, passion, memory—love. The strong emotions all came together in a kind of bittersweet pleasure as he moved inside her. His palms cupped her face and he kissed her over and over again even as their breath grew ragged.

She tasted herself on his lips.

I love you. She wanted so badly to voice the phrase that was filling every part of her, but she couldn't do it.

Couldn't take the chance he wouldn't say the words back to her. So, she shut her eyes, wrapped her legs around him and gripped the firm muscles of his butt, kneading, pulling him deeper, grinding up to meet him.

Before her own cries had quieted, she heard him cry out his own release.

How could he be both so mysterious and so familiar? she wondered, as he rolled to his back, bringing her with him so she ended up snuggled against him, her head pillowed on his chest.

SHE THOUGHT ABOUT WHAT Sierra had said. She had to be willing to apologize. Maybe she could start by having the discussion they should have had ten years ago.

She rolled over and kissed his damp chest. "That was amazing."

He put an arm around her to pull her in closer. "It's always amazing with us."

"Always has been." She shifted, laid her hand over his heart, and wrapped an arm around him.

"I—I'm…" She could do this, she told herself. She could apologize. Maybe she could even tell him she loved him. It wouldn't kill her. She took a deep breath and tried again. "Greg, I'm sorry."

He turned his head to squint at her. "What for?"

As if he didn't know. He was going to make her crawl. Annoyance spurted through her, but then she remembered Sierra's advice. If she wanted this man, she had to be willing to face her part in their breakup.

She rubbed her cheek against his chest. They were connected still, he loved her still, she had to believe that. "I'm sorry I reacted so badly ten years ago."

"Me, too."

He didn't move a muscle and yet she felt him pulling

away from her. She held on to him. "I was scared. I panicked."

"You told me I didn't trust you. That I was trying to control you."

She heard the bitterness in the words and realized he still hadn't forgiven her.

Ouch.

"I was wrong to say those things. I wish I could go back and do it over."

"We'd have a house by now, maybe a couple of kids. Instead, we're sneaking around having an illicit affair. I hate this. I thought I could do it, I really did. Have some fun, great sex, and get you out of my system. But I can't."

Her heart was beginning to pound. She realized that she was frightened on some psychic level that wasn't a place she peeked into too often.

"Please, Greg. Let's give this thing another chance. A real chance. We've both changed. We're older, more stable, maybe we understand now that what we had was too special to lose."

"I always knew it. You made a fool of me once," he said. "I can't let you do it again." He removed her head from his chest gently but firmly and unwrapped her arm from his middle. Then he got out of bed.

She could only stare at him, at a loss for words.

"I don't even know what I'm doing here. I tell myself I'll stop, but then I show up. You're like a drug I can't get out of my system, but I know there's only one way. Cold turkey."

He leaned over the bed and she saw a range of emotions struggling for supremacy. Frustration, bitterness, a little anger, but mostly she saw the sadness.

He kissed her and then pulled away with a crooked smile. "You take care of yourself."

And he gathered his clothes and left the room.

She jumped up and followed him. "Wait. Let's talk about this."

He dressed swiftly with no wasted movements. "It's too late." He opened the door. Glanced over his shoulder once, and she imagined him imprinting a last image of her. "I won't be back," he said and closed the door behind him.

"But I love you," she told the door.

She stared at the closed door for a long minute while grief built in a wave. It seemed to start in the soles of her feet and work its way up.

She didn't bother with running clothes. This wasn't something that could be pounded out of her with a few miles.

This was more important than that.

She'd lost him. He'd pretty much told her as much. But Sam had never been a quitter. And she wasn't about to give up now on the most important thing in her life.

She brewed a pot of coffee and sat in her favorite chair by the window, drinking cup after cup and planning.

When she was certain she had her idea all worked out, she called Jarrad.

"I need your help," she told him. "Yours and Sierra's."

"What with?"

"Project Romeo and Juliet."

9

THE RINK WAS BUZZING. Sam hadn't had a clue that the police and firefighter tourney would fill the Portland rink to the rafters. She'd counted on a much smaller crowd.

There must be ten thousand people here. Maybe more.

Worse, she knew some of them.

She leaned over and whispered to Sierra, sitting beside her in the section reserved for spouses and girlfriends. "I'm having second thoughts."

The woman beside her leaned over and murmured. "When you get scared, think, 'What would Juliet do?'"

"Well, killing myself on a sword seems like an easier choice than this."

"Suck it up," was the wisdom from her school-teaching mentor.

"You're a big help."

"Okay. Here. Maybe this will help bring out your inner tragic heroine." Sierra reached around her own neck and unhooked the necklace she had on. Sam had admired it earlier. An oval of pink crystal on a chain of similar crystals. Sierra leaned over and placed the necklace around Sam's neck explaining as she did so, "This is pink quartz. It symbolizes female power, healing and the heart Chakra."

She touched her fingers to the stone and found it warm from Sierra's body.

"Will it help?" She thought maybe some of Sierra's good luck in landing a great guy might at least rub off.

The woman beside her smiled mysteriously. "I don't know, but if it does I'll lend it to you again the day you marry Greg. This can be your 'something borrowed.'"

"I am so scared," Sam said in a shaking voice.

A hand reached out and clasped her own. "I know."

"I've faced misogynistic judges, crazed clients, once a cougar when I was trail running, and none of them scared me the way this does."

"It's good to be scared sometimes. It means you're out of your comfort zone."

She snorted. "I am so far out of my comfort zone I'd need a GPS to find it again."

"I have faith in you."

Sam put her hand on the female power crystal and hoped that faith and guts were enough.

Normally, she was an avid hockey fan but all she could see was a blur of bodies on the ice. Greg was there wearing his number 88 jersey, but with his helmet on he seemed more mysterious than usual. It seemed as though she'd already lost him.

"What if it doesn't work?" she wailed as the first period was about to end.

"Take off your coat and stop being a weenie," Sierra commanded.

Sam was so scared her hands were clumsy and Sierra had to undo her coat for her. Under it she wore a black cashmere sweater and her best jeans. Her makeup was flawless, her hair actually having a good-hair day and the necklace, warm against her skin, reminded her of all she had to offer Greg as a woman, as a lover, as the one person who was so deeply connected to him that she felt it would physically break her to lose him again.

She hoped he felt the same way in spite of his protests the other night.

Because she had everything riding on it.

The period ended. She couldn't have said what the score was, she'd been too nervous to keep track. The players were starting to file off the ice.

"Go!" Sierra said to her, giving her a push toward the edge of the rink.

Sam stumbled forward, realizing her hands were trembling, her knees, no doubt her inner organs were all aquiver. She was a wreck.

She wondered if the single red rose might be too much, but it was too late now. The thing was clutched in her hand and her fingers were welded shut with sweat.

She saw Greg, watched him with her whole heart. She loved everything about him. The shape of his head, the way he skated, a little bow legged, the way he smiled at her in that intimate way as though no one else in the world mattered.

The scoreboard started to flash. Jarrad had come through. Instead of a silly message to support the team or an ad, the scoreboard flashed her message.

She'd hoped that all the spectators would have bolted out of their seats to get pop or beer or take bathroom breaks by now, but it seemed as if even more people packed the rink now than when she'd first arrived.

A buzz went through the audience as people looked at the screen and then began nudging each other, whispering, settling in for a little more entertainment.

The huge screen said this:

Greg Olsen. I love you. I'll always love you. I'm ten years late, but will you marry me? I can't live without you. Samantha.

She kept reading those ridiculously huge neon words as though the message might mysteriously change. She didn't know what else to do. As a nice extra-humiliating touch, a camera had now found her, and she could see herself projected on the big screen looking like the most desperate single woman in history. She wanted to flee so badly she thought she would have if her feet didn't feel frozen to the ground. She had never, ever been so nervous in her life.

Maybe because she'd never done anything that meant more to her.

She felt like the entire world was staring at her.

Except Greg.

It hadn't occurred to her that the players would be too busy thinking about taking a break, guzzling water and doing whatever players do between periods to check out the scoreboard.

What if she'd done all this for nothing?

Then one of the fans leaned over and shouted something to the exiting players. One guy glanced up. Read the screen. Laughed. Nudged another player. More laughter.

Oh, good. She was going to be a locker-room joke. She'd never live this down. Never ever. She'd have to quit law. Move to a country where no one watched hockey, spoke English or had internet access since she could feel the number of cameras pointed her way and felt her YouTube rating going up by the nanosecond.

At last, the pushing and laughing reached Greg. She watched him turn. Felt the moment he read her words.

And then absolutely nothing happened.

He didn't rush forward onto the ice looking for her. He didn't bolt for the locker room.

He stood stock-still.

Like a rock cairn in the middle of the ice. As though he was as frozen in place, and maybe in time, as she was.

The blinking scoreboard began to look foolish. The murmurs grew sympathetic. She squeezed her eyes shut. For the first time in her life fully comprehending the meaning of the expression, she wished the floor would open and swallow her.

And then almost in slow motion, she saw Greg turn. Scan the crowd. Jarrad had appeared from somewhere and pointed to where she stood wondering if any man was really worth humiliating herself like this.

He skated slowly toward her and though she'd been frozen a moment ago, she grew hot, so hot that she thought she'd melt the ice if she stepped on it.

He stopped and removed his helmet. He was two feet away from her, the boards between them along with a decade of misunderstanding.

She waited anxiously for what he'd say. He gazed at her face with an inscrutable expression. Finally, he said, "What are you doing?"

She swallowed hard. Now was the time for the truth in her heart. "I'm putting it all on the line. Giving you my life if you want it."

A bead of sweat trickled down past his hairline and he wiped at it. "You really want to marry me?"

"Yes."

He looked at her. She'd never heard a rink full of people so quiet. "Is that rose for me?"

Oh, God, he was torturing her. "Yes." And what a stupid idea that had been.

He sniffed. "You got a ring? I bought you a ring when I asked you."

She swore silently. She'd never thought that a woman provided an engagement ring when she did the asking. But then she'd never expected to be in this position.

She tugged the old school ring she always wore off her finger. Glared at him. Enough was enough. She held it out. "And if you expect me to go down on bended knee, you can kiss my—"

She never got the last word out. He pulled her to him so hard she lost her balance. He kissed her as though he'd been waiting ten years to kiss her exactly like this.

She tasted the salt of his sweat, felt the stubble of his chin brush her. Then he pulled away only far enough to say, "Yes, you crazy woman. Yes, I'll marry you."

And then he hauled her over the barrier so they were finally free of constraint and could hold each other, full body flush against full body, kissing as though they'd never stop.

She was vaguely aware of cheering. First from Greg's teammates and the opposing team, none of whom had bothered to leave the ice and take a break. Then from a packed rink of crazy people. They were on their feet, as wild as though they'd watched their favorite team win a Stanley Cup victory.

Jarrad came across the ice to where she was in Greg's arms half laughing, half crying, and when she hugged him, he hugged her and Greg at the same time. "Glad you two finally worked it out."

Sierra was there and she had to have a hug, and then for some reason Greg's entire team needed to give Sam a hug or a kiss or simply give their buddy a hard time.

"I gotta go before the next period starts," he finally said.

"I love you," she said, letting him see the truth in her eyes.

"I love you, too. Never stopped."

"Me, neither."

"Wait!" She took her ring and picked up his left hand. The ring barely fit onto his baby finger. She kissed the finger, ring and all. And then he kissed her swiftly before skating off to the dressing room. She caught the glint of her ring as he closed his fingers around it.

What a fitting engagement ring, she realized, their high school ring. Where it all began.

As he reached the edge of the rink he turned and their gazes connected. She wondered what the next ten years held. Knew it would be interesting, sometimes stressful, but worth it. So worth it.

Then he laughed and pointed up to the scoreboard.

A new message was flashing:

He said yes! Congratulations, Samantha and Greg.

She glanced back at her new fiancé and they exchanged a wordless message of their own.

I love you.

Forever.

Juliet couldn't have done better.

Breakaway

1

"DANCING?" TAYLOR McBride let the suckitude of that word hang in the air until his agent nodded.

"On ice?"

Once more the disdainful tone. The nod.

"With a figure skater?"

This time Jeremy Barker didn't nod, he launched into sell mode. "Look, Taylor, you need the exposure. You want to get off the farm team and into the bigs? You need to get yourself noticed. This gig's for charity. A hunky hockey player and a cute figure skater team up and do a dance routine on ice. It'll be fun, make a few bucks for a good cause and you'll get yourself some profile. Also, I've seen Becky Haines in person. She's hot."

"Don't care how hot she is." Which was a lie. He was always interested in hot girls, but he wasn't about to be sidetracked that easily. "She's a figure skater. I'm a hockey player. She can be so hot she melts the rink, but I'm not going out there to make a fool of myself."

"Come on. You've seen that TV show *Battle of the Blades?* It's great fun. Put a hockey player and a figure skater together and watch them try to do an ice dance routine."

"I don't think it's for me." He didn't think it sounded like fun to dress up as a dork and prance around making a fool of himself, either, but he didn't say that.

"Look, dude. You wouldn't even be getting this chance if it wasn't for the McBride name."

And didn't that up the level of suckitude? Of course he knew that. He'd dragged the McBride name behind him like a stinking hockey bag ever since he'd discovered that he and Jarrad McBride shared the hellacious, speed-demon hockey gene. He'd tried to keep up with his brother so long as a little kid that he simply grew used to skating faster than any kid his age should. He'd learned to banish fear and keep his eye on his goal, which was to one day be bigger and stronger and faster than his brother, who was both his hero and mentor.

He'd broken his arm twice, had his front teeth knocked out at twelve, torn a rotator cuff and sprained everything sprainable, but he still came back for more.

Unstoppable, that's what they called him on ice. He might not be big like Big J, but he was fast and agile. And fearless.

And he knew, to the depth of his being, that this was his year. Goodbye farm team, hello NHL.

What really burned was that he'd spent so long trying to catch up to his big brother that he couldn't imagine heading into the big leagues and not facing off against Jarrad.

But his big brother, no more a stranger to injury than he was, had really caught some bad luck. A body check gone wrong, that's all it was. Jarrad refused even to let the team exact vengeance on the punk who'd knocked him down. But that face-plant onto the ice had cost his big brother. Maybe nobody knew better than Taylor how much it cost.

Jarrad had lost his peripheral vision, and that meant he was no use to any team. His speed, his strength, his size, none of it mattered now. He was benched.

Permanently.

And Taylor's dream of one day skating against his brother in the NHL was also permanently benched. Well, if he couldn't skate against Jarrad he could play for him, which was another reason he was determined this would be his year.

"That's why I'm saying no. It's bad enough that Jarrad's had to take up coaching amateurs now he can't play anymore. Do you think I'm going to add to the family humiliation by doing the polka in public? With a figure skater?"

"It's the waltz. You'll be doing the waltz. And it's for charity."

"I'll write them a check."

"Taylor…"

"I'm a hockey player, not some guy in sequins and a leotard floating around the ice to *Swan Lake*."

Jeremy folded his arms and put on his bulldog expression.

Taylor never liked it when the bulldog came out. Usually it meant he was about to get bad news.

"Here's the deal. A team which I cannot name—" He held his hands up before Taylor could burst into speech. "Which I cannot name, is interested in you. The owner himself asked me to get you in the charity gig. See, here's the thing. A lot of guys show promise. Not a lot of guys have Jarrad McBride for a brother. It's enough to get you a look-see."

Again, he stopped Taylor before the words could burst from his mouth, old, familiar words about how he didn't want to be noticed because he shared blood with a NHL legend. He was good. Better than good. All he needed was a chance to prove himself.

As though reading his mind, which he probably didn't need to do since he'd heard some version of the same speech a hundred times, Jeremy said, "This is your chance to prove yourself. You go out there, show you can be a good sport, raise some money for a good cause, and it buys you a tryout. What's the big deal?"

There was silence for a couple of beats before Taylor tossed himself into one of the black leather club chairs in Jeremy's office and said, "The big deal is, I don't know how to waltz."

"HE DOESN'T EVEN KNOW how to dance?" Becky Haines couldn't believe her ears. Some eager marketing genius had decided that she should ice dance with a hockey player to raise funds for charity, which seemed to her a cheap excuse for people to laugh at both skaters.

Still, there were more than a few pros that she'd be happy to press up against in the interest of charity, but they'd chosen instead a raw young redneck who hadn't even graduated from the farm team yet. Taylor McBride's only claim to fame that she could see was that he had a famous older brother.

Now it turned out the guy couldn't even dance.

"Are we sure he can skate?"

She was tired from a full day of working out in the gym, her muscles sore and her temper frayed. Which is probably why she turned on her coach/manager, Irina Katanovich, and said, "I have a silver medal hanging in a display case at home that says this is not my problem."

"Tsch," was the response, Irina's favorite when she was

irritated. It nicely combined astonishment, aggravation and "what is a world-famous Russian athlete like me doing wasting my time with this spoiled young princess?"

"This is great opportunity for you. And maybe when you fix the attitude, you will add a gold medal to the display case. Now, show me again the flip."

If Irina wasn't an absolute genius and mentor, Becky would have argued. But they both knew that Irina was a big part of that silver win. And they were both driven to do everything in their joint power to add that elusive gold medal to her collection. So, she slammed down her water bottle, huffed her way to the mat and channeled her annoyance into something productive. Improving her triple flip.

And if she had to waltz around the ice with Jarrad McBride's baby brother to raise money for a cause she believed in, she'd do it. The event was projected to raise half a million dollars through ticket sales for research into juvenile diabetes, a cause that she supposed was more important than her ego.

"He'd better get some dance lessons before we start rehearsing," she yelled once she'd landed her jump on the mat.

"You keep jumping like that and you can have anything you want," Irina replied.

"And I don't have to like it."

"Tsch."

She set herself up, ripped straight up in the air, surprising herself with the height she achieved. When she landed, she was feeling better. But not a pushover.

"And I don't have to like him."

"Tsch!"

TAYLOR WORE HIS SCOWL the way a goalie wears a face mask. It was both protection and a clear keep-away sign. The hockey equipment version of a growl.

He was running late, which he hated. But his hockey practice had gone overtime and he'd had to shower. No way he was showing up to dance close stinking of sweat.

He bashed open the door and entered the rink to find some cheesy dance music playing. A scary-looking tank of a woman barked orders in a strong Russian accent and out on the ice he watched a black-clad figure launch gracefully in the air, twirl a few times and hit the ice. As much as he thought figure skating was girlie stuff, he knew the impact of hard ice on bones and joints and tendons and he had to admire the guts of the woman out there making it look easy.

The Russian woman spotted him then called something to the girl on the ice, who eyed him up and down from mid-rink and then skated over to him. There were no rhinestones or frills on her today. She wore a black training outfit that fitted her like a second skin. Even though she was small, he could see the ridges of muscle under the deceptively soft exterior. Her face intrigued him. Pretty gray eyes, dark hair pulled back in a ponytail, delicate skin and a full-lipped mouth. But there was a toughness about her that told him not to fall for the sweet exterior.

Maybe, he thought, this ordeal wouldn't be so bad. He was about to apologize for keeping her waiting when she spoke.

"You're late," she snapped, her tone as cold as the ice beneath her. "Don't keep me waiting again."

"I was practicing," he snapped right back. "Sorry if I held up your triple Salchow." Talk about a triple sow cow. He should have listened to his gut and never come near this gig.

They glared at each other. Then she spoke again, her words pelting him like ice chips.

"You gonna stand there all day whining or are you gonna lace up?"

Muttering under his breath, he yanked his skates out of his bag and swiftly laced up.

Then he slid out onto the ice, speed skating a couple of circles around her, just because he felt like it.

"All right," the scary eastern-European woman barked, stepping onto the ice and walking toward Becky. At least he assumed that was Becky. The ice princess hadn't bothered to introduce herself. "We do a simple waltz around the ice. Places."

Taylor didn't like feeling stupid on the rink. This was his home. He was as comfortable on a slab of ice as a freestyler on a snow-covered mountain, or a boogie-boarder on water. But nobody asked a freestyler to do a dance down the mountain, or the boogie-boarder to salsa across the waves. This was stupid and embarrassing.

His scowl deepened.

Becky skated up to where he stood. Raised her brows and then put a hand on his shoulder. She held the other out in the air and he remembered that he was supposed to clasp it in his, and put a hand around her waist so he could guide her across the floor. Or ice.

But something about that determined face a good foot below his told him this gal wasn't going to be led anywhere.

In spite of how awkward he felt, and how much he already didn't like this girl, he still noticed how lithe and muscular she was. Her hand seemed ridiculously small in his.

The cheesy dance music came on again, and the coach

ordered him to move. He put a foot forward, stumbled into the woman in his arms, knocked them both off balance.

With a hiss of annoyance she pulled away. Turned to her coach. "I thought he was taking lessons."

"I did take lessons. But they were on dry land. With women who didn't hiss and spit every time I touched them."

"Tsch," said the coach. "Enough. Both of you." She came forward. Looked up at him. Her face was square and uncompromising. "We have only a few weeks to get you in shape. We will work." She glared from one to the other. "Together." She backed up. "Places."

Reluctantly, Becky came close to him again. Her clear gray eyes drilled into him. "You knock me on my ass and I will sue you. Do you even know how much this body is worth?"

Had she meant her words as a sexual dare? He doubted it, but suddenly all he could think of was that hot, lithe body wound around his, and that smart-ass mouth too busy kissing him to throw out insults.

He grinned down at her. "I bet it's worth every penny."

Her mouth opened, and, as their gazes connected, heat shot between them. Then she shut her mouth and gave him a smile women had been passing down since Eve. "Trust me, you will never know."

Just knowing he'd flustered her a little bit made him feel better, and this time when he put his arm around her waist and her hand in his, he concentrated on moving with her and the music. He'd never been one for dancing, but he was a born athlete and there wasn't a sport he couldn't pick up. He found that waltzing on ice wasn't all that hard once he relaxed.

His partner was a big help. She was already a dancer

and she had a way of sort of floating along with him so that even his missteps didn't seem to count.

By the end of two hours, he was gaining confidence. He could guide them in a circle, waltz backward and forward. Okay, it was slow and he'd given up trying to keep up with the music, but he was feeling that he might be able to pull this thing off without humiliating himself.

"All right," Irina said. "No more for today. Becky can't be late for her gym coach."

Wow. A gym coach. He wondered how many hours a day she practiced and decided it was probably more than him so he didn't want to know.

"We will work on choreography," Irina said. "And then we will begin working on the lifts."

His head shot up. "Lifts? What lifts?"

"Does no one tell you anything? You will lift Becky over your head. It is part of a simple routine but the crowd will like it."

Horror spread through him. "Lift her over my head?" He gulped. "What if I drop her?"

"Then I have you killed," his dance partner informed him before heading off the ice.

2

"I CAN'T DO THIS. I can't." Taylor sat slumped in a chair at the pub above the rinks. He'd bumped into Jarrad who had cheerfully offered to buy him a beer. But there wasn't enough beer in Canada to drown the feeling of dread in his belly. "I have to lift this girl over my head. All I can see is me dropping her and her splatting on the ice like roadkill. And there go my chances of getting into the NHL."

"Not to mention you'll have killed or maimed one of Canada's sports icons. Becky Haines's fans will tear you apart."

"Appreciate the pep talk, bro. Thanks." He took a huge gulp of beer. And almost spat it out when the Woman He Most Didn't Want to Waltz With (on ice or off) walked into the pub.

Jarrad must have seen his eyes bug out of his head for he turned to follow his gaze.

"She's cute," Jarrad said in a low voice.

"She's a pint-sized skating devil," he replied.

Becky hadn't seen him yet. Maybe he'd be lucky and she'd miss him. He slumped lower in his seat.

At the bar she put in an order, then flashed a smile of

thanks when the bartender handed her a drink. Long and sparkling, with a chunk of lemon hanging off the rim.

She turned and scanned the room and he transferred his attention to his beer. He knew the second she saw him, he felt her go still, almost heard the wheels turning in her brain whether to acknowledge him or not.

She obviously went with yes, because he saw her move toward him in his peripheral vision. He wished for one moment that he had Jarrad's vision issues so he wouldn't have to see her.

He raised his head. Feigned surprise. "Becky. Hi."

She was dressed in jeans and a sweater, stylish boots. Her hair was loose and she wore makeup. She was prettier than he'd believed possible.

For a second they stared at each other. He couldn't think of one thing to say.

His brother's voice broke the silence. "Becky Haines. Jarrad McBride. I'm a big fan."

The smile she had for his brother was friendly and easy. None of the ice chips that he was offered.

"I'm a fan of yours, too," she said as they shook hands. "I'll never forget the game against the Islanders when you scored that hat trick. I cheered so loud I was hoarse."

"Please, join us," Mr. Charm said.

"Thanks."

She sat down and then Big J joined the mutual admiration society, rhapsodizing about her silver-medal performance at the winter Olympics.

"Why don't you two get a room?" he muttered.

"Pardon?" Becky said.

"He said, 'You should have a gold medal hanging in your room,'" Jarrad hastily said.

"Hmm." He could tell she didn't believe it. She'd probably heard him fine. Jarrad was giving him the don't-be-a-tool look, but he couldn't seem to help himself. This woman got under his skin and made him snarly.

Jarrad offered her the dish of peanuts even though it was right there on the table. She shook her head.

She'd already drained half her drink. "Can I get you another?" his brother asked as if he was suddenly a waiter.

"Sure. Mineral water and lemon."

"I can't get you anything stronger?"

"I never drink alcohol when I'm training." She glanced pointedly at Taylor's half-finished beer.

He immediately drained his glass. "I'll have another pint." Even though he usually only drank one. He waved the empty mug in the air. "An even half dozen should do it. Thanks, bro."

Jarrad shook his head and ambled off to the bar.

He gestured to Becky's nearly empty glass. "So, you don't drink?" He pointed to the peanuts she'd refused. "Don't indulge in junk food." He shook his head at her. "Do you do anything for fun?"

"Fun?" She looked at him as though she'd never heard the word before. "Do you have any idea how tough the competition is in my world? The tiniest training error, the second of distraction makes the difference between a medal and falling flat on my ass during a competition. No. I don't drink. And I don't eat half the foods I love. Like ice cream and chips. I can't remember what it feels like to sleep in as long as I like, or have a whole day with nothing to do but laze around. I don't have a team who will cover for me if I flub up on the ice. I'm it. A lot of people rely on me. So no. I don't drink or snarf down peanuts in a bar."

He felt stupid. Why had he been trying to provoke her?

He understood discipline, admired it, though she probably wouldn't believe him.

Her edge was just so sharp around him. And he found he wanted to soften that hardness a little bit, especially if they were going to be stuck rehearsing together for weeks.

He glanced at her, caught her looking at him with contempt and wondered how they were ever going to get through this.

When Jarrad returned with the drinks, she smiled at him, much more warmly than anything Taylor had ever seen sent his way.

They chatted for a while about nothing much. Jarrad was a lot better at making conversation than he was and soon had Becky giggling at some of the exploits he'd got up to in L.A. Which sounded a lot more fun than anything Taylor ever did.

He noticed that Becky kept glancing around the room. Finally, he said, "You expecting someone?"

She nodded. Turned to him and said, "My—my boyfriend. He's supposed to pick me up, but he's late." She glanced at her watch. "And I need to get going. I've got an early start in the morning." She stood, hoisted her bag over her shoulder. "Thanks for the drink."

Jarrad said, "You need a ride home?"

"No, that's—"

"I'll drive you," came out of Taylor's mouth before he had time to think. He stood up. "I need to get going too."

"Thanks, but if you've had six beers you should take a cab."

Jarrad laughed. "Taylor never has more than one. He's famous for it." He glanced between the two of them, amusement deep in his eyes. "He likes to kid around."

"Oh." She seemed uncertain.

Taylor cracked a grin. Couldn't seem to help himself. "My big brother there can also tell you I'm a good driver. Come on, I'll take good care of you."

"All right. Thanks."

She lived in North Vancouver, a surprisingly suburban location he thought, but managed not to say. Maybe she lived with her folks. Or her boyfriend. He didn't like that idea so he put it out of his head.

There wasn't much conversation on the ride. He couldn't think of anything to say, and she didn't seem too interested in talking to him, either.

The next few weeks were going to be a nightmare. The idea flicked across his mind that he could tell Jeremy the deal was off, and they should find somebody else to make a fool of themselves with Becky Haines, but even as the idea materialized he dismissed it. He didn't want to analyze why, but he had no intention of letting some other beefy jock prance around the ice with her.

He pulled up in front of a house that he figured was west-coast contemporary, all cedar and glass in a neighborhood of upscale family homes and she said, "Thanks for the ride."

"You're welcome. I'll see you tomorrow."

They spoke at the same moment. "Look," she said, "this was a stupid idea. I'll tell Irina to design a simpler—"

At the same time, he said, "Would you go out dancing with me?"

He knew she'd heard him when she stopped talking in midsentence and stared. Finally she said, "Did you just ask me out?"

"Yes." Wait a minute, had he? "No." He didn't know what the hell he was doing. "I mean, I think we might do better if we went dancing somewhere without coaches or ice or this charity appearance looming over us." He shrugged, "You can bring your boyfriend if you want."

3

BOYFRIEND? WHAT BOYFRIEND? Becky stared at Taylor, dazed, until she recalled her stupid blurted comment about having a boyfriend. As if she had time. But somehow Taylor's insults about her having no life had worked under her skin and irritated her to the point that she'd invented a love life. Anything to stop from sounding as if she had no life outside skating. Even though it was true.

And, if she was honest with herself, she had to admit that she wanted some barrier between her and the—what could she call it? Not attraction to him.

She could not be attracted to a guy who was all muscle and no brain, who hadn't become successful through years of grueling effort and iron self-discipline, the way she had, but who'd managed to be born the brother of one of the most famous hockey players in the NHL and hitched himself an easy ride to fame and fortune.

No. She could never be attracted to someone like that. It was probably some kind of hormonal imbalance that made him seem so alluring. So she'd keep him at arm's length with the fictitious boyfriend.

"I don't think..." she began.

A tiny smile began to play around his mouth. He was

too good-looking, that was another problem with Taylor McBride. Way. Too. Good. Looking.

"Scared I'll step all over your toes?"

"No, it's just that—"

"Come on. I thought you were a girl who loved a challenge. Do you really want to go out there and look stupid? Or do you want to give the crowd a great show?"

"I—" She licked her lips. This was a stupid idea. Stupid, stupid. Going out dancing with him was much too close to a date. And she had this weakness for men with blue-green eyes, craggy noses and dimples. Honest-to-goodness dimples, which she hadn't noticed until he smiled at her.

"When?"

"Tomorrow night?"

She took a deep breath. "Okay."

"Pick you up at seven."

"Fine."

He grinned at her. "I'll try not to stomp on your toes."

"Don't worry. I'll be wearing steel-toed boots."

The last sound she heard as he drove away was his laughter.

She let herself into her house. The one that was such a good investment situated as it was in North Vancouver, halfway up a mountain. When her parents and she had toured the house with the real-estate agent, she'd agreed with all of them that this house was a place she could grow into. Raise a family.

"You don't want to waste that nice sponsorship money on anything frivolous," her accountant father had warned.

And, because she appreciated how much her folks

had sacrificed in order for her to follow her dream, and because he was so smart about money, she agreed.

She did like the house. A west-coast contemporary made of cedar and glass tucked in a wooded cul-de-sac, the house was much bigger than she needed, big enough that she'd been able to install her own dance studio in the basement, and leave two of the four bedrooms empty. Trouble was, she didn't have a family. She was a single woman living in suburbia.

At twenty-three she wasn't all that interested in home maintenance and gardening. She worked so hard at her sport that she sometimes wished she could flop on the couch in a nice small condo, preferably something downtown so she could spend her limited free time having fun.

For some reason, the word *fun* conjured up the image of Taylor McBride. Big and gorgeous and seemingly clueless as to how lucky he was to have been born with Jarrad for a big brother.

He wasn't her type at all, and yet she had to admit there was a strange kind of chemistry between them. She both dreaded and anticipated their evening out dancing.

The message light on her phone was blinking but she didn't knock herself out checking who'd called. She was pretty sure she knew.

After eating a meal off her menu plan, a grilled fillet of salmon with brown rice and spinach, and a big salad, she settled herself on the couch and picked up her messages.

As she'd suspected, there was a message from her mom. Cindy Haines was a bit of a control freak and it had been a struggle for her to accept that Becky needed to be in Vancouver in order to train with her coach. Sure there were great coaches in the Toronto area, where her family lived, but Irina lived in Vancouver and wouldn't budge for love or money. And Irina was the coach Becky needed.

Since she couldn't see her daughter every day, Cindy called every day. Becky loved her mom, but sometimes she fantasized about going an entire week without feeling required to give her mother a full accounting of her activities.

Every time she tried to get tough, she remembered all the times Cindy had hauled herself out of bed in the cold dark of winter and driven her to the rink for a 5:00 a.m. practice before school. All the costumes she'd provided, the skates, the expensive lessons, the trips for competitions. And so she returned the call.

Strangely enough, when she got off the phone she realized she hadn't once mentioned Taylor. Or the upcoming charity event.

TAYLOR PICKED HER UP for their dancing date a few minutes early, which she considered a good sign.

He'd dressed not like the slob he usually was, but like a sophisticated man, in a suit, no less, and his shoes were either brand-new or he'd polished them.

She wore a black cocktail dress with big silver jewelry and heeled dancing shoes.

He appeared so different in the formal clothes, and the feeling of strangeness continued as he brought out a set of good manners she wouldn't have known him to possess— opening her car door and helping her out as though she were precious royalty.

The dance club was dimly lit, for which she was grateful. Not that she was a particularly recognizable celebrity for anyone but figure skating fans, but she was known.

They settled at a quiet table in a corner where she

ordered a club soda while he had a beer. A band was playing hits from the forties.

They chatted for a few minutes about nothing and suddenly he leaned forward and captured her hand in his.
"Come on. Let's dance."

"Okay."

Somehow she'd known it would be like this when they
touched. His hands, discreetly and properly placed, one
clasping her hand and the other resting at her waist, felt
warm and intimate. When he pulled her close, she smelled
his skin and knew he could smell hers.

It wasn't that she spent a lot of time sniffing men, but
something about the way Taylor smelled made her want
to bury her nose in his neck.

The beat of the music was strong and insistent and
it was clear that his lessons had worked better on dry
land. Either that or he'd spent the past twenty-four hours
practicing. She liked the confident way he maneuvered
her around the crowded floor, the way his cheek brushed
hers.

She found her feet moving and her blood pounding to
the same rhythm. She wouldn't look into his eyes, that
would be too dangerous, so she kept her gaze on the hol-
low of his throat below his Adam's apple, where his pulse
beat slow and steady.

At twenty-three she'd had men in her life. A couple of
well-publicized romances, one with another skater who
was such an egomaniac she quickly grew tired of him, and
one with a young Canadian actor who was trying to gain
a name for himself. She'd known all along that he liked
her as much for the press she brought him as for herself
and when it ended she hadn't cried many tears. The truth
was she put so much physical energy into her skating, that
she didn't have much left for a man, or for sex.

Until now.

Had she ever felt so hot for anyone in such a short time as she suddenly felt for Taylor? No. Her relationships followed a certain predictable pattern. A few get-to-know-you dates, some kissing, and usually by then she knew if she wanted the man in her bed or not. Taking her time was important, not only for her personality but for her career. The last thing she needed was for some guy to blab private details to *eChat Canada*. So, she took her time, made sure she controlled things. All of which left her less likely to end up with a failure on her hands than someone who blundered blindly into relationships.

Dancing with Taylor, simply dancing with the man on a crowded floor, felt like throwing out all her careful methods and rushing blindly into an affair.

How had he done it?

She'd come along thinking they'd fumble around the dance floor, he'd step on her toes or bump into other couples and she'd end up giving him a lesson.

Instead, she was with this self-assured almost-stranger who had the most amazing body and the most delicious way of touching her. This was a fox-trot, for heaven's sake, not some dirty-dancing bump-and-grind, but the effect on her senses of moving with him filled her mind with images of the two of them naked and moving together.

Because this wasn't dancing. It was foreplay. Somehow this man had gone from being a barely tolerated boor to the sexiest ballroom dancer around.

Their fellow dancers were an assorted bunch. You could spot right away the older couples who'd been taking dance lessons and liked to show off their moves, and those who came because they liked big-band music, and there were a sprinkling of younger dancers too, out having a good time, taking an old-fashioned dance medium and making it new.

Taylor's big body pressed against hers as the floor grew more crowded and she felt the pulse beat of desire grow stronger.

"Did I tell you that you look beautiful tonight?" he said softly against her hair. The mere whisper of his breath stirring the tendrils was like an electric charge.

"Thank you."

Their bodies brushed as they moved, she felt the heat coming off him and her skin grew as sensitive as though he were caressing her. She heard her breathing change to the lighter, quicker breaths of arousal. What was wrong with her?

The music changed to a slow waltz. He twirled her around the floor and she thought how well-suited they were and what a surprise that was.

When the music ended, she was breathing rapidly and knew it had nothing to do with physical exertion.

Amid the applause for the band, he leaned his forehead against hers. "I think we've got this dancing thing down."

"Oh, yeah."

"You want to take a walk?" he asked, suddenly, huskily. She nodded. If he'd asked her to go home to his place and throw off all her clothes she thought she'd have nodded to that too.

They returned to their table where Taylor threw money down and then took her hand and led her out into the night. The sudden rush of cold air hit her, energizing her.

There was a current humming between their joined hands that both stimulated and unnerved her. Determined to get some idea of who he was before launching herself into his bed—assuming he was thinking about it as much as she—she marshaled her thoughts.

Behind them a quartet of Japanese girls giggled and shot each other with digital cameras.

What exactly did she know about this man her body wanted to jump all over naked, she wondered. Next to nothing.

Pull yourself together, Becks, she chided herself. *Where's your sense? Stay in control.*

They walked a little farther and she tried to take in the atmosphere of her adopted city at night; the tanker ships in the harbor twinkling with lights, across the water the north shore all lit up and the ski runs of Grouse Mountain stretching like a sparkling necklace. Her heels tapped on the sidewalks and she found this man beside her clogging all her senses.

He looked, felt, smelled and sounded delicious. She hadn't tasted him yet, but every part of her knew it wouldn't be long.

"Everyone knows about your brother, but nobody knows anything about you," she said, deciding to come right out and ask. "What's your story?"

He glanced down at her and his eyes glistened as they passed under a streetlamp.

"My story's still being written," he said, tightening his hold on her hand ever so slightly. "I hope you'll be a part of it."

Oh, come on. What was she, stupid to fall for this practiced seduction? "That's not much of an answer."

"Oh, I'll tell you anything. Everything," he said, running a fingertip down the slope of her cheek. She shivered, feeling the finger trace its path like a single raindrop.

4

BECKY LICKED HER LIPS. Tried not to notice the quiver of desire running through her body. "Tell me about your—I don't know, childhood?"

His index finger was busy, this time trailing a curve from her left collarbone to her right, leaving a trail of shivery heat in his wake. She could stop him, slap his hand away, well, she could if she had any willpower, but she didn't. She let herself be toyed with, on a street in downtown Vancouver where any gawker with a pair of eyes could see them. Where any busybody with a digital camera could film them and her little erotic interlude would be uploaded to the internet in minutes.

She was joking, but he seemed to take her words seriously.

"My childhood was great. We had a pretty traditional family. My mom worked part-time as a nurse, which was a good thing with all the injuries in our family. Dad worked in forestry. He was a big, strong guy and he loved hockey. We lived on a lake and when it froze, we'd all be out there. He was the one who got us into the sport and I never saw him prouder than the day Jarrad got drafted."

He paused for a second. "We lost him a couple years

back. A major heart attack. My mom moved to Victoria so she's not too far away, but not too close either. She still nurses, gets over when she can.

"I don't know what else to tell you. I played a lot of hockey, hung out with the guys," he said, his eyes seeming dark and mysterious in the dim light from the street. "Kind of like now. Except that now, I get to do grown-up things."

He stepped closer and her heart jumped. "Like this," he said softly, maneuvering her into the entrance alcove of an upscale apartment building. "The adult kiss," he said and covered her mouth with his.

As his lips touched hers, lust slammed into her, flattening her the way Taylor's body flattened hers against the thick glass door. She clutched at his shoulders, feeling at once overwhelmed and triumphant. He might be trouble, he might be a little rough around the edges, but she couldn't stop her attraction to him. Her skin tingled as he pressed against her, her mouth opened under his and he thrust inside with greedy haste but with a finesse that surprised her. Giving in to the inevitable, she wound her arms around his neck and kissed him back.

This wasn't an experience she was ever going to forget, she thought dimly as he took her mouth with the kind of fierce focus she imagined he'd bring to his hockey game. And, she hoped, his lovemaking.

She was so carried away by his truly remarkable kissing, that she was only barely aware of a click and a whir.

With a startled cry, she fell backward and realized the door had opened and she'd tumbled into the foyer of the apartment building.

"What are you doing?" she whispered. She glanced around and saw a fountain wall, sleek granite floors, a couple of discreet elevators. She shook her head, trying to rattle her brains back into some semblance of order as the obvious answer to her question hit her. "You live here."

"I do." He kissed her again, deeper this time, longer. Oh, she was lost. "Do you want to come up?"

Even through the mists of lust she had to wonder at how convenient this all was. He happened to choose a dance place that was only blocks from his home? "Did you plan this?"

A low chuckle was her answer. "No plan. No. I hoped." He squeezed her shoulders in a way that could be purely friendly or wildly sexual depending on how turned-on a woman was. "But I'm an optimist."

A sensible woman would walk away now. She knew this. All her dates had been so carefully orchestrated, she'd thought through all the consequences before ever sleeping with a man. Now? She wouldn't know sensible if it skated right over her toe.

She nodded. "I want to come up."

"I am so happy you said that."

She realized there was something else she had to share, as embarrassing as it was going to be. "Um, there's something else I have to tell you."

"What is it?" Something in her voice made him wary, she could tell. She drew a breath.

"I don't really have a boyfriend." How stupid she felt that she'd lied in that infantile way. She was about to explain when he kissed her.

"I know."

"How do you know?" Was she so wretched that he'd figured out right away she was manless? What was this, a pity date?

"I called Irina. Made conversation and skillfully extracted the information that you are single."

She was beginning to realize that Taylor was a lot tougher than he appeared. Still, her jaw dropped in shock. "You called Irina?"

"Sure. Why not?"

"My coach Irina?"

"Yep, that one."

"You bothered her at home?"

"Yeah. She's our coach for this gig. She's getting paid."

In the years she'd trained with Irina, Becky could only remember calling her at home once, when she'd had flu so badly she couldn't stand. Her fever was stratospheric, her head ached as though a demon was inside her skull with a jackhammer and chills shook her. Still, she'd contemplated showing up for practice rather than call Irina at home so strongly had the woman warned her that she did not like to be bothered when she was not working.

"And you called her up out of the blue to interrogate her about my love life?" Annoyance began to creep into her tone. Not to mention a sense of betrayal. Wasn't Irina supposed to be her personal coach? What was she doing giving out information about her private life? "And she told you anything you wanted to know?"

"It wasn't quite like that." He gazed behind her shoulder at the fountain wall as though it might have a few answers. "Look, why don't we go upstairs and I'll tell you everything?"

"Because you'll distract me. I prefer to know right here and right now how badly my coach betrayed my confidence."

"She didn't, exactly. Okay, I kind of sucked up. I called her to tell her how fantastic I think she is and to ask her for some advice on lifting." He sighed and looped his hands around her neck. "Because the honest truth is I'm scared to death I'll drop you."

"You won't. We'll work it until you get it right. I promise."

He didn't look completely convinced, but he left the subject alone. "Anyhow, I said your boyfriend must be a lucky guy and she said you didn't have one."

This did not sound like Irina. "She said, I don't have one? That's it?"

"No. It was more like that weird noise she makes, like a chicken choking on birdseed, then she said—imagine this with a heavy Russian accent—'Becky is not so foolish. What time has she for men?' which I took to mean, no, you don't have a boyfriend."

"Oh."

"So who were you waiting for in the pub that night?"

"Another figure skater. Jason. He sometimes drives me home, but his practice went late and he forgot."

"Lucky for me," Taylor said and kissed her again. By the time he was done she felt as liquid as the wall of water. "So, why did you pretend you had a boyfriend?"

His eyes were as blue-green as her fantasies of the Caribbean, and when he turned them on her she felt weak-kneed.

"Because I wanted to prevent this, I guess." And she reached up to brush his jaw with her lips.

"Nothing was going to prevent this," he said. "Not from the first second I saw you and you started bitching at me."

She'd have argued that it was his fault she was bitchy since he'd arrived late and swaggered in as if he owned the rink, but her mouth was too busy kissing him to be able to talk.

They got to the elevator somehow, barely breaking

contact. And then they were inside the small space riding up.

He felt so good, so strong and solid and too amazingly sexy. She wanted to devour him and it was obvious he felt the same. He kissed her, using his lips and tongue and his whole body, so she felt kissed everywhere. His hands were in her hair, on her shoulders, running down her arms and then brushing across the tips of her breasts, almost by accident but not quite.

"You feel amazing," he said against her mouth.

"So do you," she whispered back.

The elevator deposited them somewhere in the middle of space and she couldn't have said what floor they were on or which way they turned, all she knew was that she could not get into his apartment, or his bed, fast enough.

When Taylor dropped his keys as he fumbled open the door, she smiled to herself, happy he obviously felt as off-center as she did.

He scooped the keys up, opened the door and the two of them fell inside, wrapped around each other once more.

"Oh," she said, when she noticed the floor-to-ceiling windows. "It's gorgeous."

"Tour tomorrow," he said, walking her backward in a way that reminded her of their routine on the ice. This was a kind of dance too, she realized, moves of seduction and retreat, arousal and uncertainty. Now that she was here, retreat was too late, uncertainty banished. All she felt was need and heat, blistering heat that drove her on.

He pushed open a door, danced them both through it.

She was pressed gently back onto a big bed that dominated the room, and she let herself fall. Oh, those big, hockey-stick-wielding hands could entice her skin. The kiss became a full-bodied affair and from the impressive erection nudging her belly, she knew he was as aroused as she. Their breathing grew harsh.

Outside, down below on the streets of downtown Vancouver, late-night partiers wandered, and she'd hear snatches of shouted conversation, the honk of a car, the muted roar of a bus going by, but in here it was private, dark and intimate.

Her sighs sounded loud. When his hand began to draw her skirt upward, she felt every inch of her thighs hum with pleasure.

She slid her thighs apart because she couldn't help herself and the small move unleashed a wild coming together of mouths and tongues and bodies so fevered they grabbed and rubbed and pushed closer and closer until their clothes felt like heavy armor.

She was so hungry for him she shocked herself. His hands were on her back, slipping around the front to rub her breasts, in her hair, gripping her hips, while his mouth was busy at hers, so hungry, so demanding.

"Oh," she said, tilting her head back. "Oh."

His mouth was busy at her shoulders, her neck. Drowning her with needs and emotions she couldn't keep up with.

"I need you," he said raggedly. Not *want,* but *need.* She knew exactly what he meant.

"Oh, yes," she answered, knowing now that this had been inevitable. From the first moment she'd seen him, big and unkempt and gorgeous, she'd recognized an attraction more powerful than any she'd ever felt.

"Every time I hold you in practice, I want you," he muttered, his hands sliding into the silk bodice until he touched her breasts. They ached for him and when he eased the fabric down so that she was naked to his gaze, she reveled in the freedom. Now he could see her, her skin so pale under the moonlight sliding in the uncurtained window. Now he could touch the breasts that tingled for him, now he could taste them. He bent his head and took one nipple into his mouth and the sensation was so strong she felt that much more would be dangerous.

"When you skate me backward?" she admitted in her turn, "I always imagine there's a bed behind me, and we'll fall into it and make love."

"It's about to happen now."

How had this happened? She never lost control like this. She was Canada's Skating Sweetheart but she felt more like Canada's Skating Sex Addict.

And if she didn't get a fix, she would die.

"Can I make a request?" she said in a low voice she barely recognized as her own.

"Anything, sweetheart."

"Do you think I could see you naked?"

5

TAYLOR HAD PROBABLY felt this good in his life before, he simply couldn't remember when that might have been.

"Oh, yeah, I think I could do that for you," he said, leaping off the bed and grabbing at his shirt to yank it over his head.

"No," she stopped him. "Slowly. I want you to take your time."

"I don't know how much time I've got," he said, but he did his best. He felt strange taking his clothes off as though it was a spectator sport, but at least the lighting was low so she didn't have to know how completely she'd got to him.

He felt her gaze on him as steady and fixed as a spotlight and he wanted so badly for her to like what she saw. Normally, he didn't give his body much thought, but she was so small and perfect that he felt like an overgrown gorilla in comparison.

What if she hated hairy chests? He had no time for guys who shaved them, but maybe that's what she liked? He tried to gauge her expression, but it was hard to tell what was going on behind the eyes that watched him so intently. He felt enormous, like a big lumbering giant, and his cock, which he'd always been secretly proud of, felt too big. She was all muscle, but her frame was small. What if he hurt her?

He got down to nothing and stood, feeling all of a sudden foolish and uncertain.

She didn't help. Looking at him like he was some new species she'd never encountered before.

Maybe they could fool around for a little bit, and he could give her time to get used to his size. Make sure she really wanted an oversized ape in her bed.

Then she spoke.

"You are even better naked than I imagined." She did not sound like she was scared or revolted or turned off. She sounded like a hot woman who could handle every hairy inch of him.

And his momentary lack of confidence vanished like a puck disappearing into his opponent's net. Slam. Gone.

He stepped back over to the bed and slipped a hand to her knee. And then higher. She huffed out a helpless sigh and let her thighs part for him. He took his time, teasing his way up, higher, slipping the silk up her thighs so she would feel the cool air on her skin. Her panties weren't more than a scrap of silk and lace, but it was kind of a turn-on being buck naked while she was still fully dressed.

He played his fingers over the silk, and found it warm and damp with her arousal. She arched up against him, making a tiny sound in the back of her throat. He said in a conversational tone—as cool as he could manage under the circumstances, "Do you mind if I take these off?"

A tiny, helpless moan slipped out of her mouth. The corners of his mouth kicked up, but that was the only indication he gave that he'd heard her.

He looked down at her and her eyes were alive with

anticipation. They were going to be so good together. Sometimes you just knew.

He wanted to take his time but need was stoking him. He hooked his thumbs under the little strings at the side of her panties and eased them down.

He slowly stroked his way up her inner thigh. Her skin was so soft and velvety. There was a tiny mole on her inner thigh that he had to stop and kiss.

"I don't want to mess up this pretty dress," he said to her. "Do you think we could take if off?"

She nodded. No words at all, simply a nod. He liked the idea that he'd robbed her of words.

She sat up and together they peeled the black dress over her head. To his shock he discovered there was no bra under there. Wow.

Her breasts were small and perfect. He loved the muscles of her, taut under her soft skin. The glint of the heavy silver pendant against her delicate body, more flashes of silver at her ears and wrist. He ran a hand down from her shoulder over her breasts, her belly, to her hip.

"You are perfect," he told her.

"No, I'm not."

"Shush." Because she was, to him she was absolutely perfect and he wasn't taking any arguments.

He settled down beside her, "Now, where was I?"

In answer, Becky opened her legs wider, shocked at her own forward behavior. Usually she let the guy lead, but somehow, with Taylor she enjoyed their back-and-forth bossiness. It worked on the ice and she had a feeling it was going to work really well in the bedroom.

Besides, she was throbbing with anticipation to feel his fingers play over her. She could see his hands as she'd watched them so many times, sturdy, capable hands that could stick-handle a puck down the ice and into the net but could also touch her with such sensitivity. He seemed to hover over her neediest place, and then, when she expected him to stroke her, he ran his fingers through her curls as though checking for tangles. He stroked and patted, and then, when he delved deeper to where she was slick and needy, her hot button already quivering, it was a shock to find him touching her there, stroking her, stoking her.

Desperate. Had she ever been so desperate for a man in her life? It was as though every minute they'd spent together had been foreplay for this moment. She was so ready she thought she'd fly apart the second he touched her.

She wanted to hold on and enjoy every exquisite moment as he stroked her, obviously taking pleasure in her growing excitement, encouraging her with soft words until she shattered against him.

Her urgency slaked, she wanted more, she wanted all of him. But she didn't have to tell him that. He was already reaching for his nightstand drawer.

A rip and a rustle and then they were kissing, more hungrily than before. His skin was warm against hers. His heart beat a crazy rhythm. Unable to wait another second, she climbed over and straddled him. He was a big man, but she was lithe and fit and her body had never felt so athletic, so perfectly tuned for action, as it did at this moment.

He felt warm and very, very hard when she grasped him in hand. He made a tiny sound, a man at the end of his rope, a feeling she knew well. Her body was stretched over him, eager and wet and so very hungry.

As she positioned him at the entrance to her body, their gazes locked. She saw the glow of his eyes in a face that was surprisingly serious. He'd always seemed to her like a carefree, everything's-for-fun-and-why-bother-getting-stressed kind of guy. But as she'd come to know him through practice she realized she'd misjudged him. He worked as hard as she did, was equally intent and focused when they trained. It was only when the work was done that he let his crazy fun side out.

But this wasn't the crazy fun guy. This was a man letting her see into his depths. She tried to be as brave and held his gaze with her own as she lowered herself slowly onto him.

"Take it easy, sweetheart," he said softly. "I don't want to hurt you."

Would he hurt her? Maybe. She realized it was a chance she was taking, but he wasn't hurting her physically. Not at all.

Oh, she realized it had been a while and he was a big man. The stretch was amazing. Delicious. He seemed to go on and on, filling her completely. When they were locked, hip to hip, she took a moment to savor the deep connection, kissing him as though she'd never stop and then need took over. She moved on him, slowly at first as she accustomed herself to him, then faster as instinct and desire stronger than anything she'd ever known gripped her.

Her silver necklace, an expensive designer piece she'd bought herself after her medal win, danced between them. For a crazy moment she imagined this as a medal performance and knew they were going for gold.

His hands were all over her, squeezing her breasts, tracing the lines of her belly, grabbing her hips. Her thighs gripped as she rode him in a frenzied rush. They kissed deep and hard and with little finesse. He grabbed her hips at last when the thrusting grew so wild he had to hold on to keep up. She heard panting and knew it was hers.

He muttered words of encouragement, some incoherent as passion built.

Then their words were lost as they kissed deeply and hungrily, the bed bouncing in an age-old rhythm, as they launched each other over the edge of the world.

"Oh," she managed. And she slumped over him, damp and spent.

She felt his mouth kissing her shoulder, his hands stroking slowly down her back. For a long time they stayed like that, bodies still connected, hearts thumping while they caught their breath.

She felt the way she did when she was launched high in the air and knew that every part of her was in perfect harmony. As though she could fly.

6

"No one can know about this."

Taylor blinked open sleepy eyes, still heavy from last night's pleasures.

Never at his best in the morning, he ran his tongue over his teeth. Blinked a few times. Said, "Huh?"

Becky looked adorable in the morning. Tousled, her face pinker on one side where she'd slept on it, a little redness on the upper slope of her breast making him feel bad that he'd given her whisker burn.

She followed the direction of his gaze then yanked the navy cotton sheet up to hide her breasts from his gaze, which seemed kind of cruel. "I said, no one can know about this," she repeated.

Where was the passionate, incredible woman of last night? He heard the same ice-princess tone that she'd treated him to the first day they'd met.

But underneath that, he also heard urgency and appeal in her voice and wondered what the big deal was.

It's not that he was planning to take out an ad in the *Vancouver Sun* or plaster their exploits online. And he wasn't the kind of guy who boasted in bars.

He reached over and put his hand over hers where it

clutched the sheet. "Not the first thought I had when I woke up." He watched the pink bloom deeper under her fair skin. He leaned closer, put his lips to the soft place under her jaw where a pulse beat. "Want to know what my first thought was?"

A tiny purring noise emanated from her throat. She'd surprised and delighted him in the night. Not that he'd been sure what to expect. She was so tense and angry a lot of the time, and yet, once they'd started dancing last night and begun treating each other like actual human beings, like two people, both young, healthy and open to whatever, she'd relaxed. More than relaxed—she'd warmed to him with a speed that was both flattering and that made him wonder what her regular life was like.

Her lips began to curve even though her gaze remained fixed on the tangled bedding. "What?"

He watched her, feeling an answering tug at his own lips. "I was thinking," he said, tracing a finger across the top of the sheet where it crossed her breasts, "I was thinking about how I'd like to repeat everything we did last night."

Her gaze flicked up to meet his and he saw sexual heat flare, then her gaze dropped again. He loved that she seemed a little shy this morning. Not at all like the open, giving woman she'd been in the darkness.

"I don't have the energy," she said.

He'd reached the crease where breast connected with underarm, so he tracked down, following the plump slope, dragging the sheet down with his hand. She resisted only the tiniest bit and then with a sigh let go so the sheet fell to her waist. "I bet you do."

Her body was a perfect combination of athlete and woman, both muscular and curvy.

He leaned forward, licked across her nipple making her

sigh. "I love every square inch of you," he whispered, licking again. "No. Make that every curved inch of you."

She giggled and then as though she'd lost a fight with herself, relaxed against him. "Don't you have to be somewhere? Practice or something?"

"Nope. You?"

"Not for a few hours."

"All right then. Let's fool around."

"That sounds so seductive to me," she said, sounding wistful rather than turned on.

"I do my best."

"No, I mean the concept of fooling around. I hardly ever do. My schedule is packed, my diet is controlled, some days I feel more like a machine than a person."

This wasn't anything he hadn't already noticed, and he suspected his personal mission in life was going to be to help this woman relax. "When you are in my bed, you are all woman."

She giggled again. "I think you are very bad for me."

"I disagree." Then he pulled the nipple all the way into his mouth and they were both too busy to talk any more.

WHEN SHE WOKE FOR the second time, Becky stretched, feeling the delicious pull of muscles that didn't get used all that often. And her body was so toned that there weren't many muscles in that category, sadly only her intimate ones.

She looked over at Taylor who was sleeping with his mouth partly open and a shaft of light arrowing across his chin where she could see the stubble forming.

The sheet was tangled around one ankle, and one hairy leg stuck out.

While he was asleep, she indulged her urge to explore.

His body was both mystery and delight to her. Who'd have thought this big hairy jock would have such a delicate touch or that he would be so intuitively sensitive to her needs?

It wasn't that any of her previous lovers had been awful, but that Taylor was in an entirely different category. She thought that he genuinely loved women and his pleasure in her body and her mysteries and her responses only fueled her own pleasure.

Somehow, his utter lack of any inhibition lifted her own and she was able to be bold, to take chances. Normally, she saved all her boldness and risk-taking for the ice. In the past she'd let the man in her life take the lead sexually. But with Taylor she was almost forced to tell him what she liked, what she wanted, since he asked so many questions. Naturally, that opened the door for her to ask him. Once he'd even taken her hand and shown her exactly how he liked to be touched. It was one of the most erotic experiences of her admittedly limited sex life.

She traced her fingers softly through the springy hair on his chest, tracked the ridges on his belly. There was a bump on one arm—from an earlier break she assumed.

His hands were so big compared with hers, she stroked her fingers over his, then she eased the sheet down over his waist so she could really see the part that had pleasured her so last night. She discovered it was moving. Thickening and lengthening before her eyes. She glanced up swiftly to find Taylor regarding her with lazy, but nevertheless carnal amusement. "You taking advantage of me while I was sleeping?"

She grinned up at him. "Actually, I was exploring."

"Yeah? See anything you like?"

She liked all of it. But she didn't want to feed an ego that already seemed overfed. "I was counting your scars."

He snorted. "Take all day."

"How did you get that?" she asked, running her fingers over the bump on his arm.

"Coming off an outdoor rink too fast. I was about ten." He rubbed his fingers over where hers had been. "Pissed me off because it meant I missed the rest of the season."

"This one?" She traced her finger over a jagged scar on his calf.

"Skate. Happened in junior high."

He rolled her over, pinned her, as though suddenly tired of the game, or of her nosy perusal of his body using the excuse of scar-counting. "How 'bout you? Bet you don't have any scars, being a figure skater."

Even though she knew perfectly well he was being deliberately provoking so she'd let him explore her body in exactly the way she'd explored his, she decided to rise to the bait. "Oh," she spluttered, "I've got scars, buster."

"Yeah? Let's see 'em."

She pretended to hesitate. "One's in a very embarrassing place."

Speculation fueled his gaze. "You don't say?" He scratched his chin, letting his gaze wander lazily over her body. "Not your breasts. I made a pretty thorough inspection."

"Not my breasts."

His hand started to slip over her breasts, lower to her belly. "Could I discover it by feel?"

In spite of the fact that she'd had more sex in the last twenty-four hours than she'd had in years, her body purred to life again.

His lips followed the path of his fingers and she let herself enjoy the sensations spreading over her skin.

"Here?" he murmured against her belly, running his tongue over the faint line.

She chuckled, feeling her skin vibrate against his lips. "That was appendicitis. Not very exciting, though it did get me out of a geography test in high school."

"But not the embarrassing scar."

"Nope."

The exploration continued, and he was a very thorough explorer. Between them they catalogued cuts, breaks, pulled tendons and the assorted damage athletes do to their bodies.

"Aha," he said at last. "So faint I almost missed it." He had her flipped on her stomach and was tracing a finger over the middle slope of her buttocks where a faint scar remained.

"What happened?"

"I was seven. In one of my first competitions." She smiled at the memory. "I was wearing this pink and purple costume with sequins that my mom made me. My hair was in ringlets, of course, and there were matching pink and purple ribbons in my hair. Everything was going great, and we had a final warm-up before the comp, and Keili Munro tripped, right into me, so we both fell, and then Russell Cartright skated into my butt."

"Sounds painful."

"More embarrassing, honestly." She shrugged. "And I sure was upset that I couldn't compete. But I had to go get stitches." She glanced back at him. "You get used to pain."

He nodded. Rolled on his elbow and asked, "Do you ache every day?"

"Yeah, mostly. Especially when I'm training hard. My joints and tendons take a beating, I've had tendonitis in my Achilles, more sprains than I can count. It's part of the process. You?"

He seemed a little uncomfortable answering, as though

wishing he'd never brought up the subject. Finally, he said, "Yeah. But you get used to it."

"It's part of the price of fame," she said with a twist of her mouth. "And speaking of fame, no one can know about this."

"Are we back to that?" He yawned widely. "What are you so scared of?"

"I'm not scared. It's…complicated."

"You know, I always think when people say things are complicated it's because they don't want to make tough choices."

A huge sigh escaped from her mouth. She regarded him for a long moment. "You are smarter than you look."

"Well, that's a relief."

He was so adorable she had to lean over and kiss him. As she did so she laid her hand on his chest and could feel his heart thump reassuringly beneath her palm. Because it felt so good, she left it there.

Maybe he was right and she was conflicted. But a person who'd devoted their entire life to one goal didn't start straying from the path because of a gorgeous face and body.

Did they?

"I have certain expectations," she began slowly, not sure how to phrase what she needed to say.

"Uh-huh," he encouraged her after she'd stayed silent for a while.

"One of them is that my…dating life is carefully controlled. I have a certain image."

"Sure. You're Canada's Skating Sweetheart. I know that. Everybody knows that." He shrugged. "It's like any nickname, though, right? It only rules your life if you let it."

"Not exactly. I have a kind of PR machine. Sometimes things sort of get set up for me."

"What kind of things are we talking here?"

"Dates. Men."

"You date for public relations? You're kidding me."

She shook her head. "Not kidding."

"You give everything to your sport. I'm only now getting an idea of how many hours a day you put in. You eat a strict diet, you do public appearances. Don't you want one thing in your life that's for you? Nobody else but you?"

"Of course I do. But it's not that easy."

"Explain to me why you can't tell your PR machine to shut down on this one issue. To leave you to live your private life in peace."

"Because I don't get to manage everything."

"Sounds like you don't get to manage anything."

She spluttered with indignation. "You don't understand. How could you possibly know what it's like to be me?"

He appeared interested in her sudden outburst. Pushed an arm behind his head and regarded her. "Why don't you tell me what it's like to be you?"

7

BECKY ROLLED OFF Taylor's bed, suddenly needing movement to help her formulate her words. She paced, not realizing or not caring that she was naked, "My parents gave me everything. Our entire lives from the time I was three revolved around my skating." She glanced at him. "I was a natural. The tiny tots figure skating class got me hooked. I loved everything about it. The slippery ice, the sparkly costumes." She made a wry face. "The applause. The teacher was pretty well-connected with the skating community and she talked to my parents."

"You were three?"

"Yep. Of course, there was no guarantee that what she thought she saw was really there. But my parents were pretty thrilled with the idea that their little girl was special. So they sent me to more classes and then the private coaching started when I was five."

"You have to start young."

"I can't even tell you how much money my parents have invested in me. In skating, and in tutors so I stayed caught up in school. And the time they've spent driving to rinks when it's still dark out, cheering me on in every competition. Our family holidays all revolved around my competition schedule." She shook her head. "It's been crazy. So, now that it's all finally paying off, I feel like I owe—" She stopped herself. "No. Not owe them. I think they've earned the right to help manage my career, even—"

"Nobody has the right to manage your love life," he interrupted. "Only you."

"You don't understand," she said again.

"The hell I don't. You think I don't have natural talent?"

She laughed. "Of course I do."

"It runs in my family. Sure, Jarrad got it first, but I got plenty of my own." He grinned suddenly, slyly, very much the younger brother. "I'm faster than him."

"Really?"

"Yep. He can shoot harder and his aim's probably a bit better, but I'm faster. It's my gift."

"Cool."

"But here's what I've noticed, and maybe because I watched Big J go through it I saw it clearer than most. When you have talent, a lot of people want a piece of that. It's a dream. Maybe my kid's the next Gretzky. And they see the headlines and the money and the celebrity life for their kid and they get hooked too.

"And you don't think coaches are looking for the future champions? And agents? All those people who want to help a talented kid, they aren't a bunch of philanthropists, you know."

"Of course I know that. But if you're saying my parents want me to succeed because they want money and fame, that's simply not true. Or fair. You don't even know them."

"I know what they've done to you. You're what, twenty-four?"

"Twenty-three."

"Twenty-three and you have to go out with whoever they tell you to?" He gazed up at her, the usual humor absent. "Honey, that is way out of line."

"I— They love me."

"I believe you. Doesn't mean they know what's right for you. I'm only saying, maybe you don't have to pay them back for all those skating lessons with your life. Maybe being Canada's Skating Sweetheart doesn't mean that everybody in the country owns you, either."

"I think—" At that moment her cell phone shrilled. She dug it out of her bag, giving him a very delicious view of her backside. She pulled out the phone. Went completely still for a second and shoved it back in her bag.

"You didn't answer. Hmm. Another guy?"

"No." A slight flush mounted her cheeks.

"Your coach?"

"None of your business."

"Good old mom and dad?"

"Oh, shut up. Okay. Maybe I let them have more influence than I should. I'll think about it." She began to search for her clothing. Stepping into panties, finding her dress on the floor. "I should get going."

"I could buy you breakfast." He rolled out of bed, came to stand behind her, kissed her bare shoulder. Then glanced at the clock. "Or lunch."

She shook her head. "Thanks, but I've got stuff to do."

She was stepping into her dress and when she had the shoulder straps on, he pushed her fumbling hands away and zipped her up, enjoying the smooth line of her back, the sad reverse of the moment when he'd first unzipped her.

"Can I see you again?" he asked.

Her body went momentarily stiff. He probably wouldn't even have noticed had he not been standing with his hands resting on her shoulders.

Suddenly she turned. Gave him a bright smile and reached up to kiss him. "Of course you're seeing me again. Practice. Tomorrow."

Then she grabbed her shoes, her bag and ran lightly down the stairway.

He followed at a more leisurely pace. "Wait. I'll drive you home."

"Oh." She stood rooted to the spot beside the front door where in some foolish attempt to stamp his own personality on the condo, he'd installed a pop machine. It was obvious she'd forgotten she didn't have her own wheels.

"I could get a cab."

"Please let me drive you home. I promise not to beg you to see me again or embarrass you in any way."

She squinted her eyes at him as though suspecting a trap. "Promise?"

"Yep. We'll talk about the weather. Have you noticed that it rains all the time here?"

A hint of a smile appeared. "Okay. Thanks."

So, she was going to make this difficult was she? Deny them both a fully satisfying relationship because of some bogus PR crap about whom she could date.

Putting aside the fact that he thought he was good dating material, he suspected he was going to have to get rid of whatever pretty boy they'd set up for her.

He flexed his fingers as though about to don his skating gloves. There was nothing Taylor enjoyed more than a challenge.

BECKY THREW OFF LAST night's clothes and jumped into the shower in a mix of so many moods she wanted to smack her head against the shower tile to try to knock some sense into herself. Her body still hummed with repletion, and little phrases uttered, images caught, flashed through her mind making her hot all over again.

Then there was the real life she was trying to live. The one where she had a public persona, responsibilities, where her romantic life was taken care of by a PR department that included her parents, but which certainly left her a lot freer to concentrate on her skating career.

Or life. Maybe that was the problem. Skating had become her entire life.

When she emerged from the shower the land-line phone was ringing. She ran for it. Checked call display eagerly. When she saw it was her mother, an absurd sense of disappointment hit her. Gagh. What was wrong with her? Did she seriously think Taylor was going to call her within half an hour of dropping her off? After she'd pretty much blown him off, making it clear she wasn't available.

This, a voice in her head chided, *is why it was better not to get involved with men.* Unfortunately, the voice sounded a lot like her mother's.

"Hi, Mom," she said, picking up the phone.

"Hi, baby. I called earlier, where were you?"

She hated lying. To anyone. But especially to her mom. "I was in the shower," she said, which was true. Not when her mom had called, but she hadn't exactly told a whopper.

"Oh, you must have got an early run in. Good for you. You are so dedicated."

Well, not answering wasn't lying either, was it?

"So, how are you and Dad?"

"We're fine. More than fine. Really excited in fact."

"You guys finally going to take that cruise?" she asked

hopefully. Her folks had been talking about a cruise for years but kept putting it off, usually because of her.

Her mother laughed. "No. Not this year. Not with so much happening. The good news is for you."

For some odd reason her stomach tightened. "What is it?"

"How would you like to go to the Grammys?"

"The Grammys? You mean the music awards?"

"Of course, those Grammys."

"Do they want me to be a presenter or something?" It sounded like an odd request, but she did get some strange ones. The idea flitted through her head that it would be fun to present a music award, but the vision was wiped out by her mom's next words.

"Not as a presenter, honey. As the guest of one of the nominees."

"Which nominee?"

"Cory Slater! They're calling him the next Michael Bublé."

"I know who he is." A slight, blond boy from Vancouver Island who was probably her age or a couple of years younger, he was the latest young male singing sensation. After putting out a debut album that had taken the music world by storm and excited way too many 'tween girls, Cory Slater was obviously going places.

"He's going to be famous, soon everyone will know who he is."

"Why would I go as his guest? Is he a figure skating fan?"

"No. It's for the publicity. For both of you. Being seen with him will be good for your image. He's clean-cut, sings classic songs, none of that rude rap stuff. Hopefully some of your fans will start listening to his music.

We might even try to use one of his songs in one of your routines, but we can talk about that later."

"And what do I get out of it?" Apart from yet another guy supposedly dating her who wasn't interested in her any more than she was interested in him.

"He's going to be huge. It will bring music fans to you. And it shows that you're a multifaceted young woman who knows about more than simply skating."

"I don't know, Mom."

"You've got a couple of months. We want you two to get to know each other a bit first. Be seen at a few public venues. Let the word out to a few key media and bloggers. They call that viral marketing," her mom said. Becky doubted her mother would know viral marketing from Michael Bublé, but she kept her mouth shut.

"We thought this Friday would be perfect. You can go out for dinner at one of those places where celebrities are always being sighted, and then maybe out dancing."

"No. Not dancing." The thought of doing with Cory Slater what she'd done last night with Taylor McBride was unthinkable.

"What is it, honey? You sound tired. Are you eating properly? Taking all your vitamins?"

"Of course I am."

"Maybe I should fly out there this weekend. It's the Morrisons' twenty-fifth anniversary party, but I could skip that. We could spend some time together. Go to the spa."

"No. I'm fine,' she snapped a little too quickly. "You go to your party. Honestly, everything's fine."

"Well, if you're sure. I'll send you the details about Cory Slater. He says he's really looking forward to meeting you."

"But—"

"I've got to go. I'll call you tomorrow, sweetie." And her mother was gone.

And Becky had a blind date set up by her parents.

8

"HOW FAR APART DO YOU want us to be for this section?" Taylor asked. They'd been practicing a couple of hours on a small piece of the dance routine. They hadn't started lifts yet. He wasn't nearly ready for that. But he was starting to feel pretty comfortable with the dance steps. Irina might come off as scary but she was a good coach once he got used to the accent and the way she barked orders. He began to realize it was her way of speaking, not that she hated him as he'd first assumed.

"That's my job," Becky informed him tartly. "Basically, I do most of the work. You stick to your moves and don't screw up and we'll be fine."

He threw up his hands. "Okay, boss." She was right, of course. She was doing the bulk of the ice dancing while he faked a couple of Fred Astaire moves and then did a few lifts. The lifts terrified him. He'd skated a few times with trophies over his head, and some of them were heavy, but he'd never tried to carry an actual living person. What if he dropped her?

He was having nightmares at the thought.

That's when he wasn't dreaming about her in entirely different ways.

Not that any of those dreams were coming true either. Since their one night of fun he'd kept things strictly business. If there was a pulse that beat between them when their bodies touched, she couldn't blame that on him since at least half the heat was coming from her.

If their eyes sometimes connected for too long, or their hands stayed clasped a few seconds more than strictly necessary, he didn't figure that was all him either.

He didn't think one time was going to be enough for either of them. But he could wait until she knew that as well as he did.

He might not wait patiently, but he'd wait.

And then they started the lifts.

Irina showed him what he had to do. He would lift Becky and she'd arrange herself like Ginger Rogers spinning around a ballroom dance floor with Fred. All he had to do was hold her up and skate in a circle.

They practiced first in a gym. It wasn't too bad and she didn't weigh much.

Then they moved to the ice.

He prepared to lift her, she skated to him and he grabbed her, but didn't lift. "I can't do it. What if I drop her?"

"Do not drop her," Irina said, at her fiercest.

"You won't drop me." Becky looked at him, giving him an understanding smile. "If I start to slip, I'll cling on like a monkey. Hey, I trust you."

Somehow, her confidence rubbed off on him. He took a breath. Figured even if something happened he could angle his body to take the fall. "Okay. I'm ready."

She skated up to him, he caught her in his arms, lifted her. She was so agile, so strong. He felt her move, changing position, felt their bodies align, let his skates lead him in circles, trusted her, trusted him, trusted them together.

The last part of the move was her sliding slowly down his body to land on the ice, where she'd spin away. But they hadn't got to that part yet. All he had to do was let her slide down his body.

Relief spilled through him as they made it through the lift, and then she was sliding down, into his arms. When she reached the ice, her arms wrapped around his neck and her body snug against his, she gave him her generous smile. "You didn't drop me."

"I didn't drop you."

And because the relief was so enormous, and she was so sweet and the imprint of her body was a reminder of everything they'd done together, everything he wanted to do again, he lowered his mouth to hers.

A sharp intake of breath, part warning, part sigh, and then she melted against him, kissing him back with all the pent-up longing he'd hoped she suffered.

"Tsch!" Irina burst out.

He ignored the coach. "Come out with me tonight," he murmured against Becky's lips.

"I can't."

"Sure you can. I'll take you somewhere where no one will know you. A dark, secret place where the paparazzi never go."

"Your place?"

"No. My favorite pool hall."

Her laughter bubbled. "You're asking me to play pool with you?"

"I am." He figured she had enough idiots asking her for fancy dates. Anyone could see she was a physical kind of woman who didn't want to sit around all night eating a bunch of crap that wasn't good for her athlete's body.

"I've never played pool." She sounded interested.

"Excellent. I'll teach you. I'm a very good teacher."

He moved in closer. "A very good teacher."

"We are talking about pool, right?"

He grinned at her wickedly. "What else would I be talking about?"

She shouldn't go, Becky knew that on every level. A date, even as non-date as playing pool sounded, could give the man the wrong idea, plus she had her set-up date the following night with Cory. She needed to look her best.

But rebelliousness kicked in. Why shouldn't she have some fun just for herself? Who was she hurting? Besides, she reasoned, the more time she spent getting comfortable with Taylor, the better their routine would turn out to be.

"Okay," she said. "You're on."

SHE DIDN'T KNOW WHAT she'd expected. A pool hall, she supposed, with slit-eyed characters betting large sums of money on sinking some ball into some pocket.

In fact, Taylor drove her to a neighborhood pub in Kitsilano named Jason's. Jason's had been around for forty years and if there'd been an update in decor during that time the redecorating was too subtle to notice.

Downstairs were big TV screens showing several sports at once, scarred wooden tables that were about half-full. The clientele was a combination of university students and locals, some of whom looked as if they'd been coming here since the place first opened.

Taylor led her up a flight of wooden stairs and there was a single pool table sitting under lights.

One more TV screen played up here, and a quartet of students battled it out noisily over a dartboard.

Becky put down her bag and approached the table. Her life had been so narrowly focused on one sport that she'd never even held a pool cue, never mind tried to hit a ball. She had no idea what she was doing.

Taylor, however, had clearly misspent a lot of his youth around pool tables. He pushed some coins into the slot, set up the balls in a triangle and removed a cue from the wall.

He explained that she had to shoot the white ball into the triangle and break it up. Sounded easy enough.

He bent over and she liked the easy way he moved, shivered a little when her mind flipped back to their night together when he'd taken her with the same easy athleticism he now turned to a pool table.

Once the balls were spilled all over the green felt, he came up behind her. Put the pool cue in her hand, showing her how to hold it. "Now, lean forward, put the heel of your hand down, and your fingers propped like so." He showed her how to make a V of her thumb and fingers and prop the cue in them. "Like sighting down a rifle.

"Now, prop your chin right over the cue," he instructed in her ear.

She shifted. How did he make this all sound so sexy? Maybe it was the way he felt he had to stand right inside her personal space to teach her.

"And ease your legs apart a little bit."

A tiny moan escaped her lips. He'd said those words, those very words that night, and suddenly she felt she was back there, parting for him, giving herself to him with a glorious abandon she'd never allowed herself before.

She eased her jeans-clad legs apart,

"That's good, baby," he whispered, and she knew he'd deliberately replayed the tape from that night. Once more he'd repeated his exact words.

"Stop it," she said, but so breathlessly it didn't come out as any kind of order.

"Sorry," and he swiftly kissed her lips.

Neither of them noticed that one of the dart players was suddenly taking more interest in them than in the dart game. Or that he'd pulled out a small camera.

Matt Frenshaw was a third-year journalism major who worked on the college's student paper and also worked as a freelance stringer for the *Vancouver Province*. He'd recognized the two right away, not thinking there was much of a story there until he saw that kiss. So, Canada's Skating Sweetheart was recruiting from the farm team, was she? He could see the headline now. He crept downstairs to make a quiet phone call to the city desk.

As the lesson progressed, Becky found herself enjoying the challenge of lining up her eye and the cue and drawing an imaginary line between the pocket and the ball. It was sort of like geometry, the only math she'd ever been any good at. After an hour or so she was sinking a few of the easy shots and suddenly, to her horror, another couple came up and challenged them to a game. They didn't seem to care that it was her first time out and Taylor was soon chatting with the guy as though they were the oldest friends in the city not two complete strangers.

"Okay, honey," he said, after the four had introduced themselves, "Come over here and have a strategy session."

Strategy session? All she was going to try to do was not make a fool of herself or get in the way.

"Now, this is real important, when you go to shoot, let that scoop on your top flap open a little bit. Throws the guys way off their game."

"You'd better not look, then."

"It's different for me. Because we're on the same team. That gives me a home-team advantage."

She shook her head. "You really are that guy, aren't you?"

"What guy?"

"The guy who looks down women's tops."

"Honey, every straight man is that guy." And he patted her backside.

Fortunately, Taylor was so good at pool that her lack of experience didn't matter too much. And she even managed to sink two balls during the three games, which thrilled her.

After the games, they all shook hands and she and Taylor left. They got into his car and he started the engine. He sent her a look that melted her bones. "Where to?"

Okay, so he'd been seducing her all night, they both knew that. Those little touches, the compliments on her natural aptitude as a pool player, the way he always seemed to brush her body when he moved past her. The look in his eyes when they rested on her.

Every part of her felt warm. Kind of bubbly. He was giving her that look again, that sexy, half-sleepy sort of expression that reminded her of rumpled sheets and soft sighs.

In response, she leaned over, took his mouth with hers. Kissed him thoroughly. "Your place."

"You are my kind of woman."

9

How could her "date" with Cory have been anything but bland after a night of passion with Taylor?

Cory was nice enough. He picked her up in a limo and took her to a fabulous restaurant where she drank a rare glass of wine and, even though she tried to eat sensibly, wondered how many extra pounds of her Taylor would have to heft in practice.

A reporter from *eChat Canada* had conducted a brief on-location interview with them outside the restaurant, and she knew it would air as part of an in-studio interview the singer had already taped. The piece was scheduled to air the next day. The whole thing just made her feel tired. She didn't want to date Cory.

She wanted to date Taylor.

Cory seemed as if he'd either done some research on her or had it done, as he asked her questions based on her biography and skating career, which was sweet if a bit tedious.

She, in turn, asked him about his music career and so they got through the evening without a single awkward pause or a spark of romantic interest on her part. Or his, she suspected.

After dinner, the limo returned and he dropped her off properly at home. Outside her place, he walked her to her door and kissed her cheek when they reached it.

"Thanks for a great evening," he said. He actually sounded as if he meant it, but then she had to remember that he was new to this celebrity business. After a few years, he'd probably find it a little irksome. Of course, if he really did become the next Michael Bublé, he was going to have a lot more heat than she ever would.

"You're welcome."

He shifted from foot to foot. "So, are you okay to go to the Grammys with me?"

"If you're sure?"

"Yeah. Sure. Why wouldn't I be? Okay. I'll call you." And he was gone.

She knew the piece was airing the next day, but didn't bother to watch. She'd long ago lost the thrill of seeing herself in the media.

She'd have assumed her mother had also, so when she called, saying, "Did you see the piece on TV?" Becky was surprised.

"No. I—"

"Well, you'd better take a look at it, young lady, and call me right back." And her mother slammed down the phone. It had been some time since she'd been called *young lady* in that tone of voice. Something seriously strange must have happened.

eChat Canada would repeat in an hour, but in the meantime she turned on her computer and checked Google. She typed in her name and Cory's and, to her horror, a whole pile of hits showed up. She clicked the headline of a gossip blog: Skating Star in Love Triangle with Crooner and Hockey Jock.

"Oh, no," she moaned as she clicked the link. A photo

came up of her and Cory looking pretty cozy, and he was quoted in the *eChat* interview as saying she was his muse and that he was writing a song for her. Oh, gag.

But below that was a less professional but distressingly clear photo of her and Taylor taken while they were playing pool. No way they could claim "just friends" when the photographer had caught them locked in each other's arms, kissing. And then a second photo that clearly showed their faces. She frantically thought back to that night, but all she remembered were the couple they'd played against. If they'd recognized either of them, they hadn't said anything. Had they then rushed out to call the media? But no, she and Taylor had left first.

Only then did she remember the students playing darts.

And every one of them probably had a cell phone equipped with a camera.

Covering her face with her hands didn't really help. Her palms became a kind of screen on which played the pool evening. Her secret night out with her lover. Which had nothing to do with her so carefully orchestrated dating life.

She picked up the phone. Dialed.

"Hey, sexy," Taylor's voice was laid-back, as though nothing was worth getting in too much of a bother over.

"Have you seen the news?"

"If there's another oil spill, don't even tell me. I swear—"

"It's not an environmental disaster," she snapped. "It's a personal one."

The sleepy sexy voice changed in a heartbeat. "Becky, what is it?" He sounded so adult, so concerned, so much like a man she could lean on, that for a second she wished he were here so she could press her head against his shoulder where she'd hear his heart beating and indulge in a hearty bout of tears.

"Watch *eChat Canada* and call me back."

"I hate that stuff."

"Well, then look up you and me and Cory Slater on Google."

"That weedy little singer? That is not a trio I want to be part of."

"Too late. You already are."

"Hang on." Then she heard him say, "Jarrad. Lend me that fancy phone of yours, will you?"

And after a few minutes he was back. "Well, shit. You couldn't have picked a real man as my rival?"

"Taylor, it's not funny."

"I know it's not. I am seriously pissed that you would think that pretty-boy singer is better for your publicity than me."

"What are we going to do?"

"I don't know. Don't you have people for this sort of thing?"

"I guess. I don't think they're really talking to me right now."

"Well, get hold of them. Don't say anything to anybody. I'll talk to Jarrad. He's good at this kind of stuff. He kind of got used to it after being married to that stuffed bikini. I'll call you later."

"I'm sorry."

"No biggie." And he was gone.

HER PHONE STARTED TO RING. She didn't even bother to check her call display. Her mom, Cory, Cory's people, media, friends, skating people. She didn't want to talk to any of them.

She dropped her cell phone on the table. Wrapped up

warmly and got into her car. The day was cold, the sky leaden and a light drizzle sent the damp right into her bones.

She drove aimlessly for a while, wondering how somebody who'd always tried to do the right thing, to be as close to perfect as hard training, discipline and an iron will would let her, had blown everything up.

Canada's Skating Sweetheart had become Canada's Skating Slut.

For maybe an hour she drove without any destination through North Vancouver, over the bridge and into Burnaby, and after a while, she found herself at the rink.

It wasn't her normal practice time, but she needed to be here for some reason.

"Hi, Frank," she said, checking in at reception.

"Hi, Becky."

"Any chance of a free rink?"

"Sure. Number three's open. You've got a couple of hours."

"Thanks."

She laced up, stepped onto the smooth ice. She was all alone. No coach, no audience, no music. Nothing but her and the ice.

Her blades carving ice was the most familiar sound in her world. The shushing sounds soothed her. She skated faster, letting warmth build in her muscles, feeling her lungs begin to accommodate to the motion.

All her greatest moments had happened in rinks, and some of her worst.

Even as she had the thought, she realized that a couple of her greatest moments ever hadn't been at the rink. They'd been in Taylor's arms.

With a groan she realized she'd gone and fallen in love

with a big, hairy hockey player. And that her actions would have lasting consequences on her career.

She was flying around the ice. This was her medium and she owned it. If her rising star was about to plummet, would she really care?

She already had a silver medal. Nobody could take that away, or the person she'd become while she'd trained so hard and worked so tirelessly.

But somewhere in all of that she'd lost who Becky Haines really was.

Maybe it took Taylor shaking her out of her comfort zone to make her see that she wasn't Canada's Skating Sweetheart. She was a woman, with a woman's needs and feelings.

She also happened to be a damn good figure skater.

She set herself up for a triple lutz/double toe, landed it like a champ. Threw in a double axel/double toe at the end because she felt like it.

Then suddenly, she wasn't alone on the ice. Taylor was there.

He skated up to her. "I thought I'd find you here." He lifted her chin so he could look at her. The knowledge that she loved him made her suddenly shy, but still she couldn't resist gazing into his eyes, seeing the man she'd come to care for so deeply in such a short time.

"You look different," he said. "What is it?"

She could continue to play a part or she could stand up and be the woman she'd only discovered.

She decided she had enough guts to be honest.

"I figured out I'm in love with you."

Shock wiped his face clean of expression as though she'd pushed a button and turned off a computer screen. Then a slow smile began to build, spreading from his lips to his cheeks, crinkling his eyes.

He picked her up and swung her around, and they were both laughing and panting when he finished.

As he gazed at her, he said, "I knew when I first met you that you were going to be trouble."

"Does that mean you love me too?"

He scratched the side of his face. "I guess so."

Naturally, such truth-telling involved a lot more kissing. Finally, she came up for air.

"Did Jarrad have anything to say?"

"A whole lot. Most of it older-brother bull. But he had a pretty good solution."

"What's that?"

"Something that's pretty close to the truth. That we fell in love during this skating thing and you didn't want to hurt Cory's feelings."

"So I was two-timing him?" She didn't like that notion at all.

"No. In Jarrad's version, that night you two went out for dinner you told him that you were in love with someone else. And because the interview with Cory had already taken place, it aired. Big J's already got hold of Cory. He thinks that if Slater's willing to play it our way that everybody can win on this one. And you'll get to be Canada's Skating Sweetheart again."

A smile began to bloom. "I don't care about that."

He kissed her. "You don't?"

"No."

"How would you like to be Taylor McBride's sweetheart instead?"

She grabbed his hands and skated in a circle, pulling him with her. Then she threw back her head and laughed in sheer joy.

"I love that plan!"

Epilogue

"I HAVEN'T BEEN THIS nervous since... Oh, hell, since you were a rookie," Samantha said to Jarrad. They were in the VIP box with plush seats offering a perfect view of the ice where Taylor McBride was about to make his debut appearance as an NHL rookie. None of them were sitting in those plush seats.

And the delectable array of food and drink set out was going untouched.

"I don't think I was this nervous when I was a rookie," Jarrad agreed.

"I'm not nervous," Becky said. To her shock, she wasn't, either. "Taylor was born to do this, just like you were. He's been training and dreaming of this day since he first stole a pair of your old skates and toddled onto the frozen pond and fell on his face."

Jarrad laughed. "He told you that story, huh?" He leaned his forearms against the rail and stared out at the blank white ice the way a sea captain stares out into the sea. "You're right, Becky. Even if he falls flat on his face tonight, he's still living the dream."

Sierra put a hand on his shoulder, the diamond from her engagement ring sparkling in the light, and Jarrad's much bigger hand automatically settled atop hers. "I know how much you both wanted to play in the league together. I'm sorry."

Jarrad turned to her and kissed her swiftly. "Honestly, I'm not. He's spent enough of his life in my shadow. This is his time. Soon nobody will be referring to Taylor as my little brother. They'll be talking about me as the brother of Taylor McBride."

Becky knew that the two brothers had spent some hours the night before talking about the game and reminiscing about their childhood on the ice. Taylor had told her that Jarrad had given him the best advice a former NHL star could give a rookie. "Everybody's going to be watching you. Don't try to be a hero on your first time out there, don't do anything stupid and you'll be fine."

"Five minutes to game. I need something to pass the time. Anybody got a deck of cards?" Jarrad asked.

Samantha and Greg exchanged glances. She spoke up. "No, but I've got some news that should take your mind off Taylor."

"I doubt it," but he turned and gave his sister his full attention anyway.

So did Becky and Sierra. Greg pretty much always gave Sam his full attention so that didn't count. With a flick of her long, dark hair, Sam said, "We're inviting you all to our wedding."

Even though they'd declared their love in public, Sam and Greg had been pretty tight-lipped about their engagement. Greg refused even to call it an engagement and though he continued to wear Sam's school ring on his finger, she didn't have a diamond of her own. Becky had noticed and had hoped that everything would work out okay for these two strong-willed, stubborn people.

Seemed as if she'd worried for nothing.

"'Bout time," Jarrad said, echoing her thoughts. "And don't forget Sierra and I are getting married next spring. Don't mess that up, will you?"

"Not at all," Greg said. "We're getting married next month. In Hawaii. We booked everything. A great resort, a minister and we're keeping the guest list to family and a few really close friends. All you guys have to do is show up."

"Hawaii? Wow. But what about Taylor?" Becky had to ask.

"Don't worry. We've worked the wedding dates around his schedule."

"But Sam doesn't even have an engagement ring." Becky felt she should bring it up. She liked traditions and Greg and Samantha seemed to be messing with a lot of them.

Greg made a rude sound. "This woman's only getting one more ring from me. Last time I gave her an engagement ring it didn't go so well."

"Oh, shush up," Sam said to her beloved. Then she turned to Becky. "I'm having one ring, but it's gorgeous. We designed it ourselves." She shrugged. "Seemed appropriate."

"Two McBride weddings in a year." Jarrad glanced at Becky with one of his way too good-looking smiles. "What would be totally cool is a hat trick."

Every eye in the VIP box turned her way, but luckily she could hear a commotion behind her. "Shhh," Becky said. "The players are coming on the ice." And she couldn't have been happier for the interruption. Then she turned, her heart in her mouth as she watched the players skate onto the frozen surface. When Taylor made his entrance, their VIP box cheered loudly, and they weren't alone. He was already a popular rookie; between the family connection with Jarrad and his own charm, people wanted him to do well. No one more than Becky.

He acknowledged the crowd as though he'd been doing it forever, then turned and faced their box. He raised a hand to his family, palm flat and fingers slightly spread, and Becky felt her heart turn over. She lifted her hand and mirrored the gesture.

They weren't ready to share their love with the world— or their families—quite yet. But they were talking already about their futures, fitting their careers around their personal life, where they'd live, how many kids they wanted. She'd even caught Taylor eyeing trays of engagement rings when he thought she wasn't looking. Becky liked the sound of a wedding hat trick.

She liked it very much.

COMING NEXT MONTH

Available March 29, 2011

#603 SECOND TIME LUCKY
Spring Break
Debbi Rawlins

#604 HIGHLY CHARGED!
Uniformly Hot!
Joanne Rock

#605 WHAT MIGHT HAVE BEEN
Kira Sinclair

#606 LONG SLOW BURN
Checking E-Males
Isabel Sharpe

#607 SHE WHO DARES, WINS
Candace Havens

#608 CAUGHT ON CAMERA
Meg Maguire

REQUEST YOUR FREE BOOKS!
2 FREE NOVELS PLUS 2 FREE GIFTS!

red-hot reads!

YES! Please send me 2 FREE Harlequin® Blaze® novels and my 2 FREE gifts (gifts are worth about $10). After receiving them, if I don't wish to receive any more books, I can return the shipping statement marked "cancel." If I don't cancel, I will receive 6 brand-new novels every month and be billed just $4.24 per book in the U.S. or $4.71 per book in Canada. That's a saving of at least 15% off the cover price. It's quite a bargain. Shipping and handling is just 50¢ per book in the U.S. and 75¢ per book in Canada.* I understand that accepting the 2 free books and gifts places me under no obligation to buy anything. I can always return a shipment and cancel at any time. Even if I never buy another book, the two free books and gifts are mine to keep forever.

151/351 HDN FC4T

Name _____ (PLEASE PRINT)

Address _____ Apt. #

City _____ State/Prov. _____ Zip/Postal Code

Signature (if under 18, a parent or guardian must sign)

Mail to the Reader Service:
IN U.S.A.: P.O. Box 1867, Buffalo, NY 14240-1867
IN CANADA: P.O. Box 609, Fort Erie, Ontario L2A 5X3

Not valid for current subscribers to Harlequin Blaze books.

Want to try two free books from another line?
Call 1-800-873-8635 or visit www.ReaderService.com.

* Terms and prices subject to change without notice. Prices do not include applicable taxes. Sales tax applicable in N.Y. Canadian residents will be charged applicable taxes. Offer not valid in Quebec. This offer is limited to one order per household. All orders subject to credit approval. Credit or debit balances in a customer's account(s) may be offset by any other outstanding balance owed by or to the customer. Please allow 4 to 6 weeks for delivery. Offer available while quantities last.

Your Privacy—The Reader Service is committed to protecting your privacy. Our Privacy Policy is available online at www.ReaderService.com or upon request from the Reader Service.

We make a portion of our mailing list available to reputable third parties that offer products we believe may interest you. If you prefer that we not exchange your name with third parties, or if you wish to clarify or modify your communication preferences, please visit us at www.ReaderService.com/consumerschoice or write to us at Reader Service Preference Service, P.O. Box 9062, Buffalo, NY 14269. Include your complete name and address.

HBI I

"You were right to turn my marriage offer down," Aristedes said.

And Selene found her voice at last, found the words that would not betray the blow he'd dealt her. "Thanks for letting me know. You didn't have to come all the way here, though. You could have just let it go. I left yesterday with the understanding that this case is closed."

Before the hot needles behind her eyes could dissolve into an unforgivable display of stupidity and weakness, she began to close the door.

The door stopped against an immovable object. His flat palm.

"I can't accept that." His voice was low, leashed.

What did her tormentor mean now? Was he ending one game only to start another?

She raised eyes as bruised as her self-respect to his, found nothing there but solemnity and determination.

Before she could voice her confusion, he elaborated. "I never let anything go unless I'm certain it's unworkable. I realize I made you an unworkable offer, and that's why I'm withdrawing it. I'm here to offer something else. A workability study."

She leaned against the door, thankful for its support and partial shield. "Your son and I are not a business venture you can test for feasibility."

His gaze grew deeper, made her feel as if he was trying to delve into her mind, take control of it. "It's actually the other way around. I'm the one who would be tested."

She shook her head. "Why bother? I know—and *you* know—you're not workable. Not with me."

His spectacular eyebrows lowered over eyes she felt were emitting silver hypnosis. "You're right again. Neither you nor I have any reason to believe that isn't the truth. The only truth. It might be best for both you and Alex to never hear from me again, to forget I exist. But then again, maybe not. I'm only asking for the chance for both of us to find out for certain. You believe I'm unworkable in any personal relationship. I've lived my life based on that belief about myself. I never really had reason to question it. But I have one now. In fact, I have two."

Find out what happens in
THE SARANTOS SECRET BABY by Olivia Gates,
available April 2011, only from Harlequin Desire.

Harlequin Blaze

red-hot reads

Sunny, sensual Hawaiian spring break…again!

Three best girlfriends are recapturing an amazing spring-break vacation they had a decade ago.

First on the beach is former attorney and all-around good girl Mia Butterfield. Meeting up with her boyfriend of old is a bust, so she's shocked when her hero turns out to be someone she'd never have expected…

Find out who it is in

SECOND TIME LUCKY

by acclaimed author

Debbi Rawlins

Available from Harlequin Blaze® April 2011

Part of the sensual miniseries,
Spring Break

Part 2: Delicious Do-Over (May)

Harlequin®

A *Romance* FOR EVERY MOOD™

www.eHarlequin.com